HAVING YOU

The Carrington Chronicles

A. C. Arthur

"When I saw you I fell in love,
and you smiled because you knew."
– William Shakespeare

PROLOGUE

Turks & Caicos
1 Month Ago

"Come to my room with me," he said, his voice as smooth as the surface of the water behind him.

I could only stare for the next few seconds because this was only the third sentence he'd spoken since approaching me on the beach where I sat. My legs were partially spread—the thin gossamer fabric of my multi-colored sarong wet from my giddy run into the water twenty minutes earlier—sticking to them like a second skin. My hands were still planted in the sand as I'd propped myself up so I could look out to the waning moon as it glistened over the dark sheen of the ocean. My bikini top was too small, a testament to the last time I'd been able to enjoy time at the beach, or even a pool. My ample breasts all but toppled over the swatches of coral material. Unfortunately, it would have been too obvious if I yanked on that top a little bit to sort of save myself some pride.

Instead, I continued to look up at him, at this gorgeous hunk of man that had just happened along the beach on the night when I had a few moments of free time to be on the beach as well.

Score one for fate.

"Are you serious?" I asked eventually because he hadn't said another word and something told me he wasn't going to, not until I answered him anyway.

I don't know who he is or where he came from.

But like I believe I said before, he's gorgeous. He's very tall, over six feet, with a muscled physique that brings actors like Vin Diesel or quite possibly Duane Johnson to mind. His clothes hung perfectly on him, as if his personal tailor considered muscles and bulk no problem at all. With a close-shaved head and a neat goatee, his lips drawn tight, and knotted brows, he has a solemn air about him, even though I'm sitting on the beach scantily dressed at well after midnight.

"I'm always serious," was his reply. "I'm staying in the Desire Penthouse. We can be there in about ten minutes."

Again, I don't know what to say which is kind of ironic since I'm studying to be a linguist and just landed my first lucrative job as a professional translator. Ronnel Mendoza, a Filipino billionaire businessman hired me from an ad I'd put online four months ago. He's paying me $20,000 a month to assist him in a major business deal by helping to translate at all his meetings and also assisting his two daughters—Malaya, who is ten and Rhia, seventeen—with learning enough English so that they will not be too far behind when they enter an American school in September.

This guy standing in front of me speaks excellent English and he smells good too. I push myself up, getting to my feet with his added help, as he reached out taking me by the arm. Heat pooled in that spot just beneath my left elbow spreading quickly like some computer virus intent on infiltrating my entire body.

"I don't even know you," I say, easing my arm out of his grasp. "I'm not from this island. I'm just on vacation. I will be leaving in two days."

"I am leaving tomorrow afternoon," he says. "So we have tonight."

"What are we going to do when we get to your suite?" I ask like I'm really considering this and really naïve to not know what he wants to do when we get there.

While I can safely say that at twenty-five years old I am no longer a virgin, the sexual exploits I've had in the past have been well after I know more about a guy than the fact that he smells deliciously sinful. This guy has a neatly trimmed goatee—her favorite look on a man—and there's a spot along the right side of his jaw where a muscle twitches each time I say something to him. I want to kiss him there, first.

"We're going to have sex and you're going to enjoy it immensely," he replies without so much as a blink of an eye.

My pussy pulsates. Instantly. Undoubtedly. As if it understands every word of what he said, and it agrees.

Taking a slow, deep breath, I wonder what his reaction would be if I immediately said no or that I'm not interested. Then I realize with a man that looks and smells like this that may not happen to him too often. All the more reason for me to go for it, but I pause to consider that option.

In the last two years I haven't had time to even buy new batteries for the vibrator I'd purchased a couple months after I'd arrived on campus in Rhode Island. I was only there for a year and a half before the company that offered the scholarship money went bankrupt. Then I'd returned to Maitlin, the small coastal town in Virginia where Gram and Pops raised me. I worked the next six months at the hardware store until I had enough saved for another semester because Pops' last words would forever be emblazoned in my mind.

"You'll be the first Jefferson to ever graduate from college. A success, that's what you're going to be. But don't forget to take care of your Gram. She loves you and I love her. Take care of her when I'm gone, Jellybean. Promise me you'll do that."

I'd promised and I didn't intend to let Pops down. So I worked every job I could to pay for school and to keep food and medicine stocked for Gram at the same time. Landing this job with Mendoza had been the answer to so many of

my prayers. I could finally finish school, albeit three years
after my original graduation goal. But I would finish and
once I graduated Mr. Mendoza, promised to find me a
permanent position possibly teaching in the Philippines
where he's from. So things were finally working out for me
on the professional front.

As for the personal...

"What makes you so sure I'll enjoy it?" I asked but had
no idea that's what I'd planned to say. The words just came
out and he simply took another step closer to me, until his
chest brushed against mine. My nipples hardened instantly
and the sound of the waves rising and crashing seemed
much louder, the tropical air surrounding us, much heavier.

"You will," he said, his voice lowering as he lifted a
hand, running a finger along the curve of my breast.

That finger went lower until it was between my heaving
mounds, cradled in the crevice, rising and falling as my
breaths quickened.

"And so will I," he continued before pulling that finger
free then lifting it to his lips where he made a show of
licking around the digit.

I gasped. Couldn't help it. I'd never seen anything so
simple and yet so erotic in my life.

"Condoms," I said next. "I want to see them and put
them on. That's not negotiable."

"Good," he told me. "I don't negotiate where sex is
concerned."

As he predicted, ten minutes later we were in his suite.
Plush carpet, paisley wallpaper, a glistening marble dining
room table with a huge tropical floral arrangement at its
center, a living area and then the bedroom with its perfectly
made king sized bed. That's all I saw before his hands were
on me.

The bikini top was barely holding my breasts in the first
place fell to the floor in a heap of strings. The wet sarong

followed and then the bikini bottom. I was naked in front of this stranger and instead of being deathly afraid, I was irrevocably aroused.

He looked at me then, from the tip of my head—I have no idea how the normally unruly mass of curls looked at this moment—down to my toe nails with the chipped cotton candy pink polish. Then he moved, still looking at me, and walked around to stare at my naked ass, I presumed.

I was hot all over, every inch of my body flushing beneath his silent scrutiny. There was a lamp on one of the nightstands, its light was casting a low, warm golden glow throughout the space. Enough of a glow that he probably saw the oddly shaped dark brown birthmark on my left butt cheek. Bikini bottoms always covered it, but that was on the floor now.

"Get on the bed," he directed me. "I'll get the condoms."

On surprisingly steady legs, I walked to the bed, taking a seat on its edge while I waited. He disappeared into another room, the bathroom, I suspected. When he came out his button down shirt was gone, replaced with a white tank. His pants were unbuttoned and there was a box of condoms in his hand. He came to the bed, thrusting the box at me saying, "Here, inspect them and then take one out."

I looked at him for a moment, not used to taking so many directions from someone, especially during sex. His chest was perfect, wide like a wrestler's, sculpted and honed like a fitness model. His skin was honey-toned, glistening as if he'd rubbed oil or sunscreen up and down his arms. The white pants and shirt he wore covered the rest of his body but I ached to see more, to touch, and to taste. He walked with a slow mesmerizing swagger, his buttocks tight and firm and tantalizing.

With a gulp I looked away. I opened the box of condoms and hurriedly pulled out a packet. Running my fingers over it I checked for any perforations. I was on birth control, had been for years to regulate my periods, but I wanted to make sure.

"Open it and lay back against the pillows," he said.

I opened the packet, holding the latex in my hand when I looked up at him again. His pants were barely riding on his hips now, unbuttoned and unzipped, so that the V of dark, close cut hair on his groin was visible, the bulge of his erection just out of view. It tented his pants to the point where I lost my breath.

I was hot all over, my body tingling in anticipation. My breasts were heavy, pussy lips throbbing as cream began to coat them. I was beginning to think this was a dream—a fantastically hot as sin dream.

"Lie back," he said again as he approached the bed once more.

His voice was deep, but not commanding. No, he sounded more like he was making a suggestion, a very enticing one that I knew I would not resist. I scooted back on the bed, using the heels of my feet to push me until my head hit the pillows, the condom still clutched in my hand.

He stood at the side of the bed, his hands moving slowly to grip the sides of his pants while his gaze remained locked on mine. Moving excruciatingly slow, he pushed the pants down and I couldn't help but follow that motion. His dick was as glorious to view as the rest of him. Long and thick, its mushroomed head bobbing as his legs moved to discard the linen material. Even his balls were attractive, heavy looking and perfectly symmetrical to his cock. He should have been a model, a Playgirl supermodel with every inch of his perfect face and body.

I licked my lips, heart pounding just a little faster than it had before. He climbed on the bed spreading my legs wide, looking down at my pussy as I opened. It was a good thing I'd splurged on that waxing just before the trip, a treat to myself the day I received my first payment from Mendoza.

He liked what he saw, I could tell by the gasp and then deep rise and fall of his chest that followed. He touched me too, his long fingers extending until he was brushing over my clit. It was my turn to gasp, lifting my hips off the bed at the shocking bolt of desire that seared through me at the connection. He continued his ministrations, rubbing his finger around my clit until my head was thrashing on the pillow, then moving slowly down to circle in every drop of my arousal. There was a sound, like he was milking me and I bit my bottom lip. When the tip of his finger dipped inside my pussy I felt like screaming, it was so good. So intense, so new and damn, I wanted more.

Lifting up from the pillows I boldly reached for his cock, my fingers brushing against the drop of moisture at his tip. He went perfectly still, his fingers poised inside me, his gaze lifting to mine.

I wrapped my hand around his length, loving the heat emanating there. He was so thick at the base, my fingers just barely met and I had to swallow hard again. I moved quickly, out of desperation and anticipation, to smooth the latex over him, rubbing it down his length over and over because I didn't want to stop touching him.

He moved quickly then, lifting my legs from behind the knee, pulling me down until I was flat on the bed, his dick thrusting forward, ready to enter me. My thighs shivered as I lifted my hips, wanting him more than I'd wanted almost anything else in my life.

"Look at me!" he said then, the words strained but still adamant. "Look. At. Me. While I fuck you."

I did. I couldn't do anything else.

He looked glorious, his jaw tight, eyes clouded with desire. I felt the thick head of his cock pressing at my entrance and I gasped wondering if he'd fit. I relaxed in his grip, my fingers clenching the sheets beneath me as he pressed forward, slowly at first, then with one swift push that embedded him so deep inside of me I screamed.

Not in pain, but in sublime pleasure as he filled me. He began moving immediately, circling, pulling out to the tip, thrusting in deeply, before circling his hips again. It was a wicked synchronization, a dance I felt like he'd perfected over time. And hell, it was just that, *perfection*. My entire body trembled with his movements, my mind clouding so that all I could imagine was this pleasure, all I could anticipate was the beautiful climax it promised.

I was engulfed in him, the feel of his strong arms beneath my legs, his dick inside my pussy and the low sound of his breathing as he worked. He was so controlled, so precise in the way he speared his dick inside of me, coming from this angle, pulling out and hitting another spot that made me shiver once more. Whatever he did, however he did it, he worked me masterfully and as competitive as I could be about my schoolwork, I gave everything, willingly, excitedly to him.

Everything, even the whimpers of gratitude, the seconds of asking for more and taking it as if I'd been made specifically for this moment. For this man.

My release took me by surprise with its intensity. I think I probably convulsed beneath him as pleasure rippled through me at an alarming rate. The action seemed to incite something feral in him as he moved faster, thrusting deeper, pounding into me as if it were a race to get to his climax just as fast. I bounced up and down on that bed as he moved, screams louder than I ever imagined coming from me.

I didn't care, it felt too good. Too. Damned. Good. There were no pretenses at this point. I loved how he was fucking me and I'm sure he knew it. My pussy was so wet I was positive there would be a big spot on the bed when I moved. I could hear his dick mixing in the thick coating of my desire, felt him slipping easily along the walls of my pussy.

It felt so good. So. So. Good.

He groaned when he came, a low, controlled sound as his body tensed over mine. He still held my legs and his biceps bulged, a line of sweat darkening the center of that white tank he still wore. I could feel him pulsating inside of me, every drop of his release emptying into the condom I'd applied. A small part of me sighed. I wanted that cum for myself. I'd never had a guy come inside of me and in this second I wanted his. This stranger that had fucked me so well.

He pulled out of me then, moving an arm quickly from beneath my legs, his hand going to his cock to hold the condom in place. Without a word he moved from the bed and walked towards the bathroom again.

I didn't know what to say or do so I just lay there staring at the ceiling, my body still reeling from this delicious assault.

"You can use the bathroom when I'm finished," he said tightly. "Then I'll walk you back to your room."

Because it was over, I thought after I heard the click of the bathroom door closing.

This wonderfully arousing and satisfying escapade was over.

It only took me another second to realize how definite that was. Then I was up off the bed pulling my bikini bottoms up my legs in record speed. The sarong was still a wet mess and I didn't feel like trying to squeeze myself into the bikini top. As if it had been waiting for me, the button down shirt he'd taken off was thrown over the back of a chair near the dresser. I hadn't even seen him put it there. But I'd admittedly been distracted.

I grabbed the shirt and put it on, heading out of that bedroom before the water that was running in the bathroom could stop flowing. I was at the front door of the room in no time, opening it and stepping out into the well-lit hallway. Closing the door behind me I stared back at the gold sign with the word "Desire" in black script knowing I'd never forget this place, this night, or that man.

I would never see him again I knew, but I would also never forget him or how my body had reacted to his.

THE ONE

I knew I was in love from that very first day.

There was never any question, no period of consideration, no small talk or "I need to get to know you better". I just knew.

And I want. With everything there is in me I want and need and can't wait until it's my turn to have.

I can imagine every second of when our naked bodies touch for the very first time. It will be exquisite, like drinking the finest wine or seeing the most beautiful sunset. We'll fit perfectly in every aspect, body and soul. And you'll love just as deep as I do. You'll want just as much as I do.

And we'll have it.

Just you wait and see.

CHAPTER 1

Los Angeles, California
Present Day

"Your reservation is at six. Reg will be downstairs at five forty-five," Noble King spoke in that succinct and authoritative way he had.

He stood on the other side of the desk, wearing a gray metro fit suit and skinny purple tie. In his hand was the notepad he never seemed to be without, on his face the thick framed black glasses that reminded Jerald of his middle school biology teacher.

"L.A. Prime?" Jerald asked as he stood, lifting the file from his desk and sliding it inside his leather bag.

"Perch," was Noble's reply. "French is much more subtle than steak and potatoes. Easier on the stomach when talking business, especially when that business is taking over an international company."

Jerald looked up warily. "DeMarco makes the arrangements that Jack tells him to make. He doesn't inflict his own personal desires on a professional business dinner."

Noble looked over the rim of his glasses, without a moment's hesitation. "I'm two years older than DeMarco and three times as smart." He chuckled then so as to make his remark seem less snappy then Jerald had already recognized it to be.

"Ask the professor in our business class, or simply check our references again," Noble continued as he moved around the office looking for something to tidy up, even though he knew there would be nothing out of place here. Jerald wouldn't have been able to work if there was.

He looked at Jerald matter-of-factly when he'd finished his search. "Besides, Perch has a wonderful view and great food. You'll be sitting on the terrace. Wow him with our city, order him exquisite food and excellent wine, and then take him for everything he's got. Signed. Sealed. Delivered. All before Jackson returns from his honeymoon. It'll be your wedding gift to him and that spitfire Ms. Tara."

Jerald could only shake his head at his assistant of the last three years who had come highly recommended by DeMarco Argent—Jackson's assistant who, though younger and less intelligent, was hired first. As the CEO of Carrington Enterprises, wining and dining clients was Jackson's area of expertise. Jerald, on the other hand, preferred to deal solely with the numbers, making sure the company stayed in the black.

Last weekend Jackson had married Tara Sullivan after a dangerous meeting and what Jerald had called "an intense romance". DeMarco had attempted to clear Jackson's schedule for the two weeks he would be away but this deal was too important to postpone. This apparel company had risen fast over the last ten years gaining momentum with each new line it introduced, until six months ago when reports of its owner's connection to a human trafficking ring made national news. Stock immediately began to plummet in Makisig Apparel, putting not only its warehouse in the Philippines at risk, but also the U.S. headquarters based here in Los Angeles and the other warehouse locations in jeopardy.

It was a fifty million dollar deal that Jackson wanted almost as much as he'd wanted to marry Tara. Holy matrimony won out and so the initial meeting with Makisig's owner fell to Jerald.

"Send the updated stock rankings to my phone," Jerald said lifting his bag and moving around his desk. "And the next time I tell you I want steak and potatoes, you'd better make sure that's what I get. Or, unlike DeMarco, you'll be in the unemployment line."

He moved past Noble a second or so before the door to his office swung open, a woman with fire engine red hair and brilliant blue eyes entered quickly.

"I'm so sorry, Mr. Carrington. I know you asked for these reports earlier today, but the copy machine on this floor was down. I went to the one downstairs but they're auditing some huge company down there so I couldn't cut in. I was going to try the one in the executive offices but that door was locked. So I had to wait for this one to be fixed and that just happened about a half hour ago and there were over a thousand pages to the reports so I'm just finishing. And I know you're leaving for a meeting but I can have them delivered to your apartment so you can review them when you're finished with your meeting. Or I can just bring them by myself. I know where your building is and it's not out of my way. Or I can—"

"You can stop before you give yourself a mild coronary and Mr. Carrington a migraine," Noble cut in.

He moved around Jerald to stand between him and Mandi. That was the woman's name. She was a summer intern from UCLA.

"Take the reports to my desk," Noble continued to tell her.

When Mandi opened her mouth as if she were about to speak again, Noble held up a single finger, shaking his head ever so slightly, causing Mandi's opened mouth to close with a snap.

"Just go to my desk. I'll be there momentarily and I'll walk you personally to the copy center since it seems with all your wandering about the building you neglected to find yourself in the right place."

Mandi was embarrassed, her cheeks immediately turning almost as red as her hair and Jerald frowned. He had asked for the reports hours ago and would have liked to see them before this meeting. Without another second's hesitation Mandi left the office and Noble turned to look at Jerald.

"The summer intern program was DeMarco's idea. So what were you saying about the unemployment line?" He'd arched a brow and then took himself and his notepad out of the office.

Jerald sighed. From day one Noble King had been a task, one he thought of firing about twenty times each day. But he never did, because as it turned out, the guy was pretty damned good at his job. And he had learned just about all of Jerald's OCD habits in the first week of working here, being sure to follow each and every one from that point on. So the restaurant change was out of character for Noble, but since neither of them were used to Jerald having to meet with clients, he was willing to let it pass.

Because as it had been for the last month, Jerald's mind was someplace else.

He stepped out of the shower, wrapping the fluffy beige towel around his waist and pushed his feet into his bathroom slippers. These were different from the fur-lined leather ones he wore around the apartment, as Jerald hated the thought of his bare feet on the same carpet and floors that the soles of his shoes moved across. The bathroom slippers were still of great quality leather, soft as butter, but minus the fur since he only used them when he was moving about the bathroom. The fact that his bare feet never touched the floor sort of defeated the purpose of the heated slate tile he'd insisted on being installed.

Jerald used another towel to dry his upper body as he walked into the master bedroom. The dark brown tones coupled with warmer beiges and those few burnt oranges that Lauren Asby—the designer that Jackson had referred—had insisted on. He'd originally thought the color would be too bright and would make his room look like a female resided there, but he'd been wrong. It turned out to be the warm and calming haven that he'd desired after working long, stressful hours to maintain the Carrington wealth.

He moved across the thick pile rug to his nightstand where he retrieved the remote control for the seventy-two inch flat screen mounted above the fireplace. Without a moment's hesitation he turned on the television, simultaneously activating the DVD player and signaling the disc already inside because he'd watched it this morning before leaving for work.

His meeting was at six and it was almost five now. Jerald didn't care. At this moment, as he sat down on his bed, eyes glued to the television, this was much more important.

The scene began with rolling waves crashing along the pristine beach as he stood on the balcony of his suite. He'd been practicing with the camera, making sure his equipment worked. In the next seconds she was standing there naked and beautiful. The best The Corporation had ever offered him.

But wasn't that the entire purpose of the club in the first place?

He'd only just found out about the existence of the club created to fulfil any and every sexual desire in a professional atmosphere for anyone that could afford it. Jackson had been one of the masterminds behind the sordid and lucrative establishment. Jackson had also been an active member, as he'd admitted to Jerald and the rest of their family nine months ago. To keep from bringing scandal to their family and to thwart suspected blackmail efforts of one of their enemies, Jackson sold his shares in the company and months later became a married man. A fact which made Jerald the last single Carrington.

And the newest member of The Corporation.

Jerald watched her open for him again, saw the gorgeous folds of her pussy glistening with desire and waiting, for him. His body had reacted instantly, going harder than Jerald had ever experienced before or after the accident. Even now he clenched his teeth as his dick jumped in instant response.

When she wrapped her hands around his length, sliding the latex tightly onto his rod, Jerald actually gasped, again. He'd watched this episode over and over again in the last month, until every second of activity was emblazoned in his memory, until the girl on the beach became the savior in his mind.

She was proof that all those nights he'd lain paralyzed in that bed wondering if he'd ever feel his legs again, or fuck another woman again, had come to an end. Sure, technically, the doctors had told him and his parents from the start that the paralysis would only be temporary, but Jerald had experienced his own doubts in that ten month rehabilitation period. And rightfully so, since afterwards, when the doctors had given him a clean bill of health and his family had praised every deity they knew for his complete recovery, he'd noticed something else. And he'd been devastated.

Inhaling deeply, watching as his thick length pistoned in and out of her soaking wet pussy, the sound echoing throughout his bedroom as he'd turned up the volume on the television, Jerald licked his lips, a quiet sigh escaping as he exhaled.

He'd never been harder than he had that night when he was buried deep inside her, never felt a release shake his entire body the way it had when he'd poured his cum into that condom wishing like hell it could have been shot deep inside her pussy instead.

Beneath the towel, the head of his dick poked through, eager to be inside that glorious pussy once more. But Jerald knew that was impossible. The women he slept with at The Corporation were one-time shots. Just the way he'd preferred. Even before joining the club, Jerald had functioned with a tried and true formula of professional women who recognized that sex was all they would get, payment to follow, and life moved on.

He wasn't like his brothers. There would be no marriage and family and all that sappy emotional stuff for him, fate had assured that and Jerald had learned to live with it. The recordings had come later, after he'd joined The Corporation eight months ago. Just one of the perks the club offered for his executive level membership. He found he enjoyed watching his escapades with these women, enjoyed watching the proof that after all this time he was completely healed—even though in his mind he'd still remained skeptical.

Until now.

Until her.

She trembled when she came, her bottom lip caught between her teeth, eyes closed, and fingers gripping the sheet until she'd pulled them completely from the mattress. This was his favorite moment on the video, the seconds he'd waited each day, sometimes twice a day to witness. She was a very pretty woman, her orgasm made her gorgeous and unforgettable. The way her pussy had tightened around his dick, her essence had warmed every part of him as it poured out with her release, dripping onto the sheets that he'd touched longingly later that evening, all made him want to have her again and again.

Yet he hadn't requested her. Hadn't contacted The Corporation to find out who she was or when he could see her again. It wasn't what he did and Jerald never wavered from the script. One night, one time, one release, one video. That was how he worked. That was all he needed.

Forty minutes later Jerald followed the hostess through the front entrance of the restaurant, back to the terrace level where the summer sun was still bright. He would have preferred to sit inside, not a particular fan of outdoor eating. Yet as uncomfortable as this made him feel, Jerald moved through the tables with his slow and steady gait, his shoulders squared, eyes not meeting anyone in particular through the dark lens Ray Ban sunglasses.

He took his seat and ordered a drink before accepting the menu, glad at least for the large umbrellas which had been opened and angled over the table. It provided a modicum of shade and for that he was grateful. If they were here, both Jason and Jack would have something humorous to say about him being a native Californian that disliked sunlight. They'd chuckle as they did some times when his idiosyncrasies were on full display, but Jerald would ignore them. As he had grown used to doing. He knew he was different and had allowed those differences to shape the man that he was today. The highly successful and driven man that had helped to build this company into what it was.

If he liked his ties aligned in symmetrical and color-coordinated order, so what. He had a brilliant mind for numbers and that's all that mattered when it came to counting the money brought in by Carrington Enterprises on a yearly basis.

It was with that thought in mind that he put down the menu and stood as the hostess headed towards his table, a distinguished looking man traveling right behind her. Jerald quickly buttoned his jacket once again as he stood straight, extending a hand to who he knew was Ronnel Mendoza, CEO of Makisig Apparel.

The tall, slim, man wore a sand colored linen suit and a multi-colored scarf—which was probably from the collection he'd designed—draped around his neck. His once dark hair was now heavily sprinkled with gray and cut low.

"Hello," he said to Jerald when he walked up to the table, accepting his hand for a hearty shake. "Mr. Carrington?"

"Yes," Jerald replied with a nod. "I'm Jerald Carrington. My brother Jackson sends his apologies for missing this meeting. For some reason he seems to think a honeymoon is more important than business. Go figure."

Jerald chuckled and watched as the man across from him did the same. Then his breath caught in his chest, the smile freezing in place as Mendoza stepped to the side and she looked up at him.

"This is Hailey Jefferson," Mendoza announced casually. "She will join us."

As the man pulled out the chair to the left of the one Jerald had been sitting in, Jerald searched for the words to say next. After seconds of holding his gaze, she gave a little shake of her head and then smiled—a brilliant smile that seemed much brighter than that of the nuisance sun above.

"It's nice to meet you, Mr. Carrington," she said as she slipped into the seat. She looked up to Mendoza, giving him that smile now as well as a quiet thank you.

Mendoza nodded and took the seat across from Jerald, who was still standing, frozen in that spot and still staring at her...at Hailey.

She was as pretty as he remembered. Her sun-kissed skin vibrant and smooth, eyes slightly slanted and the color of perfectly aged brandy. Her hair, the curly mass he recollected had been splayed across the pillows of the hotel bed, was pulled back from her face tonight, being held with a colorful clip just above each ear. The dress she wore was white, cut low enough in the front so that his mouth watered at the sight of the delicious cleavage on display. Jerald could easily recall how heavy her breasts were in his hands and how dark and hard her nipples became after he'd licked them.

Clearing his throat, Jerald finally moved, unbuttoning his jacket once more and smoothing down his silk tie before taking his seat. It suddenly seemed much warmer than it had been out on this open deck.

"I will say first," Mendoza began speaking moments after the waitress had taken their drink orders. "That I will not let you take my company and break it to pieces."

Jerald let the quick kick of the vodka tonic he'd order slip down his throat as he listened to the older man's words. Business would have to come first. That was a good thing, because it's what he'd been prepared for tonight. Seeing her was not.

"Your company has over five million dollars in debt. You haven't seen a profit in almost two years and orders to the U.S. stores have plummeted as a result of the accusations circulating about you and your employees," Jerald stated calmly.

He'd read the official business profile Jackson had prepared when he'd first approached the board about acquiring the floundering clothing company. There'd also been two separate files on Mendoza—one, the official business profile and the other prepared by D&D Investigations who performed all of the background checks on persons of interests to Carrington Enterprises. He knew everything there was to know about the company and its owner, and most likely some things that Mendoza didn't want him to know.

"They are all lies!" Mendoza said emphatically, before slamming his palm on the table. "They do not...there is...what do you say here?"

The man turned to Hailey then, looking at her in question.

"Proof," she said after a moment's hesitation.

She had been staring, Jerald thought with a start, at him.

"They do not have proof," she repeated with a nod to Mendoza as if she were telling him to repeat after her.

"Yes. No proof," Mendoza said looking back at Jerald with raised brows. "Lies they tell to hurt my business."

Jerald smoothed the edges of the napkin on the table. "I am neither judge nor jury, Mr. Mendoza. What I am is a businessman and when I see an opportunity for everyone to come out in the black, I take it. Now, as I mentioned earlier, your stock and your profits are falling steadily. This makes your company vulnerable for take over. Would you prefer if one of your rivals bought the company? House of Ginto, perhaps?"

The man's lips thinned, his fists balling on the table. House of Ginto was run by an up and coming Filipino designer who was taking all of Mendoza's previous business. The announcement two years ago that Mendoza's company was paying its factory workers slave wages had struck a big blow to the company. Six months after that, when the International Labor Organization working together with the U.S. Department of Labor Investigators— because three of Mendoza's warehouses were on U.S. soil—uncovered links from Mendoza and his top executives to a human trafficking ring running from the Philippines to the U.S., all hell literally broke loose. The stocks took a nose dive, stores immediately stopped shelving the two female clothing lines that catered to the working-class woman and the children's line that they had just introduced.

Jackson had been watching the company since then, paying close attention to the other companies that were also taking a hard look at the faltering organization. Jerald found himself agreeing wholeheartedly with the message his brother had emailed to him this morning. "NOW IS THE TIME TO POUNCE!"

"Angeli Reyes and his golden touch with couture designs will not only dismember your name, he will rebuild on all the design ideas you started and make them his own," Jerald continued, speaking calmly, yet succinctly as he went in for the kill. Mentioning the owner of the House of Ginto by name had pushed a personal button with Mendoza, just as he'd planned.

Mendoza frowned, his fists tapping lightly on the table so that the liquor in Jerald's glass swayed with the motion.

"And that new accessories line you just introduced," Jerald added with a nod towards the scarf the guy wore— which was, by the way, borderline hideous. "He'll take that as his own as well. Is that what you want?"

"You...you...*taong tampalasan!*" Mendoza yelled before Hailey touched a hand to his arm.

Jerald's gaze followed her movement, remembering that same hand wrapped tightly around his cock.

"*Ikaw at ang iyong kumpanya ay walang anuman kundi magnanakaw! Walang kwenta Amerikanong magnanakaw!*" Mendoza continued his rant, although this time his words were spoken through clenched teeth, his voice substantially lower than it had previously been.

When the man looked down at Hailey's hand that was still resting on his arm, Jerald felt an instant punch of jealousy to his gut. Hailey nodded at the man and then said something, in whatever language Mendoza had just spoken.

She looked over to Jerald then.

"He wants me to tell you that you are a scoundrel. That you and your company are nothing but worthless American thieves," she told him, with an almost apologetic look on her face.

So she was his translator, Jerald thought. A translator that also touched this man that had to be at least twenty-five years older than her, in an intimate way. Jerald resisted the urge to clench his own teeth.

"Be that as it may," Jerald said, keeping his eyes level with Mendoza's. "We can work together to come to amicable terms for selling your company to Carrington Enterprises. Or this entire deal can become hostile, which in light of the scandal and possible criminal charges you and your executives are already facing, you may want to avoid. I don't see that you have much of a choice here, Mr. Mendoza."

"I always have choice," the man replied in his broken English. "And I always win."

Jerald sat back in his chair then, staring at the man that had no idea he was declaring himself Jerald's number one priority to take down. Negotiations weren't his forte, but in that moment he decided he was not only going to be the one to close the deal on Mendoza's company, but he was going to do so in the most public and humiliating way he could possibly manage. And not just because the guy was an arrogant prick that needed desperately to be knocked down a notch or two, but moreso because Mendoza had just put his hand over the one Hailey had laid on his arm. Jerald definitely did not like that.

"Not this time," Jerald told Mendoza. "There's no way you can come up with the cash to bail yourself out, especially not with federal investigators breathing down your neck, and possibly only weeks away from possibly arresting you. As I stated before, selling to us is your best and most low profile offer."

"I do not care about your government. They all tell lies and do not like when another tells the same lies. I will close the warehouses here and not ship to any of your stores. How will they like that when your people lose jobs?"

Hailey gasped at that comment, looking at Jerald with concern. He wondered if she knew someone who worked for Mendoza and that's how she became hooked up with him. She hadn't struck him as the type of female that would run in Mendoza's circles, even though he had to admit to himself that outside of memorizing every inch of her body, including that oddly shaped birthmark on her left butt cheek, he really didn't know anything about this woman named Hailey.

"I think they dislike the fact that most of those workers are vastly underpaid and further undercompensated with the lack of health insurance or any other benefits coming from those warehouses, a little more. It's just the way we work here in the U.S."

"Then I will not work here," Mendoza stated.

Jerald nodded. "Then you will confine your business to the international market only? Your competitors will demolish you. Your stocks will continue to plummet and you will be forced into bankruptcy." He emptied his glass and picked up the menu. "But let's have dinner while you contemplate those options. The choice is yours," he continued with a shrug. "I'll treat you to dinner while you contemplate your options."

CHAPTER 2

"Excuse me," Hailey said only seconds after she'd finished chewing a bite of her salad and Ronnel had announced that they were leaving. "I'll just be a moment."

She needed more than a moment, but would take what she could get. It had been almost forty minutes since she'd looked into his eyes and felt that wave of desire that had ensconced her that night on the beach. Each time he'd looked at her during the dinner and strained conversation, she'd felt another jolt of lust, slapping hard against every part of her body. Her nipples had remained puckered as she inhaled the seductive scent of his cologne. And when he'd looked at her once, then down to the exposed cleavage in the low cut white dress she'd worn, Hailey had thought she would simply spread her legs right here for him.

Dammit! She'd never had this reaction to a man before and after that night in Turks and Caicos had figured she never would. But he was here and it was all happening again. Only this time it couldn't.

She couldn't possibly sleep with Jerald Carrington, one of the owners of Carrington Enterprises. Not again.

On wobbly legs she managed to move from the table and follow the hostess's directions to the ladies' room, trying like hell to keep her breathing steady and her mind focused every step of the way. She entered the bathroom barely noting the carpeted floor in the front sitting area, moving straight back to where blush colored marble countertops matched the stall doors with the wall-to-wall mirror directly across from them. Everything swirled around her as she felt dizzy and struggled to gain her composure.

Why was he here?

Why now?

Why her?

The one time she'd thrown caution to the wind and acted instead of reacting. The second she'd put her wants and needs before logic, responsibility, maturity. She knew better and had been taught by her Gram to know the man she was involved with, when the time came. Love was real, relationships were true and everlasting. Her grandparents were proof of that. Screwing a man she'd just met on a beach in his hotel room, then skipping out while he was in the shower was not smart, not by any stretch of the imagination.

Karma clearly had the same idea since she'd just spent the last half hour trying like hell not to choke on the Caesar salad while sitting less than two feet from said man.

Hailey's mind swam with recriminations and she took another deep breath, pressing a palm to her stomach in the hopes of stilling the jittery feeling centered there. She closed her eyes, trying to tell herself to count between deep breaths, to breathe slower, calmer. And then she felt someone come up behind her. Strong arms immediately slipped around her waist, warm breath touching the skin just beneath her ear as he whispered, "Go into the last stall."

Jerald's voice sent spikes of heat soaring through her body. If her legs were wobbling before, Hailey thought they might actually collapse beneath her at any second now.

"Go, before someone comes in and sees us," he urged.

Sees *him*, she thought, considering they were in the ladies' room where *she* actually belonged. She walked, no other option came to mind, pushing through the door to the last stall. The door slammed shut, lock clicking in place just as she turned to see Jerald coming towards her.

Hailey opened her mouth to ask what he was doing, to tell him this was a mistake, to say…something. The words died as his lips crashed down over hers, his tongue immediately pressing into her mouth, hands gripping her hips as he pushed her back against the wall. Hailey went with him, hands coming up to grip his shoulders, mouth opening wide, her tongue dueling instantly with his.

All thoughts of where and who they were dissipated as his hard body pressed into hers. His hands were busy, pulling up the sides of her dress, his fingers grazing over the bare skin of her stomach just seconds before pushing past the ban of her underwear to cup her bare mound.

"So slick, so smooth," he murmured when his lips moved from her mouth to nip lightly along the line of her chin. He moved down to her throat when she let her head loll back to tap the tiled wall. "Did you wax just for me?"

Hailey moaned as his fingers parted her folds touching first, her hardened clit, then moving immediately to her dripping cove. She bucked against his hands, her knees bending. When he thrust two fingers deep inside her she gasped, going up on her tiptoes, eyes wide. He was staring directly at her, eyes that had been very pale green at the dinner table, were now darker, more intense, a muscle twitching in his jaw as he spoke through clenched teeth.

"What are you doing here, so hot and wet for me?"

For him. The words danced around the haze of desire filling her mind. Had she been wet for him? Of course she had, arousal had gripped her at the throat the minute she'd seen him, all but choking the life out of her for the time she'd had to sit next to him without touching, feeling, experiencing exactly what was happening right at this moment.

"Yes," she moaned because that was the simple and soul-shattering truth. "Yes, Jerald."

She'd wanted to try his name out on her lips, to hear it in her voice for the very first time. She'd wondered. Oh how many nights had she lain in that huge bed in the bedroom at the Mendoza estate, what his name was. Who he was and where he lived?

He was here, in Los Angeles, fucking the hell out of her with his fingers.

And she was loving every second of it.

"Hailey," he sighed, lowering his forehead to rest on hers. "Sweet, hot, Hailey."

She pumped into his hand, needing desperately to get to that place, to feel that overwhelming pleasure she'd felt before, sooner, rather than later.

"Yes," she gasped as his fingers moved faster, pressed deeper.

"I want to lick you here, to taste all that delicious sweetness," he was saying, his breathing much more controlled than hers.

Hailey wanted to rip that jacket from his shoulders, to pull at his shirt until the buttons popped free and his chest was bare beneath her probing fingers. She wanted his pants off, his briefs down, his dick deep inside her pussy. On a tortured moan she arched against the wall, her pussy happily sucking at his fingers. He pumped faster, as if he couldn't stop himself. His eyes grew heavy as he continued to stare at her. She let her arms fall between them, slipping around behind him to cup his tight buttocks, pressing him into her.

"Yes!" she was moaning again, her voice echoing off the walls.

Hailey had no idea who this wanton woman was. She couldn't figure out when it had become alright for a man to follow her into the bathroom and finger her so deliciously. Her thighs trembled, her breasts aching as his hard chest leaned further into her.

"I want to be inside you. You're so tight, so hungry for my dick," he whispered.

She wanted the same thing. His every word was absolutely correct.

"Come to me, tonight. Come to me and let me end this sweet torture for us both," he talked as his fingers stroked so that coherent thought wasn't at all possible.

She trembled beneath his touch, inhaling deeply the mixture of the scent of his cologne and her arousal.

"Say you'll come," he whispered against her ear, his tongue snaking out to trace a heated path along her lobe. "Say it!"

Hailey gasped. She was going to come alright. If he just continued to pump inside her a little longer, maybe if he touched her clit again, sucked on her breasts. Oh yes, she was definitely going to come.

"Yes," she mumbled, her head falling forward so that her forehead rested on his shoulder. "Yes. I'll come."

He pulled out of her immediately then, taking a step back as if he hadn't just been finger fucking her to a pleasurable abyss. She flattened her palms against the wall to steady herself and keep from falling on her face.

"What's your number?" he was asking while Hailey was still trying to catch her breath.

She began pulling at her dress, trying to get it down her legs once more, then standing up straight. Her breath wasn't steady, her insides felt like molten lava still trying to find its way out of that tumultuous volcano.

"What?" she asked when she looked across the large stall to see him with his cell phone in hand.

He looked up at her impatiently.

"Your number. Give it to me so I can call you when I'm ready."

"Wh—when? Wait, you're going to call me when you're ready?" she asked, coherency coming slowly but surely.

"Your number Hailey," he insisted.

She paused. There was no doubt that Jerald Carrington was not asking her out on a date. No, he was asking for

another night like the one they'd shared on the island. That
blissful night they'd spent together just one month ago.

"I—" she began and heard the outer door to the ladies'
room open.

"Here," he said stepping forward and thrusting the
phone at her. "Put it in and you leave first."

Hailey wasn't sure about going to him tonight. She
didn't know how smart that would be since she was only in
Los Angeles for the summer and he was this important, rich
guy that wanted to destroy the livelihood of the other
important, rich guy that she happened to work for.

When she heard the click of a woman's heels on the
marbled floor Hailey grabbed the phone, punching in her
number before she could second guess herself again. She
had plenty of time for that later. For now, however, the last
thing she wanted was to be caught in the bathroom with
him. She pushed the phone in his direction and attempted to
move past him when he grabbed her arm.

"Don't fuck him," he whispered urgently in her ear.
"Don't you dare let him touch you. Not one more time."

Embarrassed. Angry. Offended. All of the above flew
through her mind and her body like a torrential storm, and
she yanked her arm from his grasp, escaping from the stall
before he could say another word. Or incite another wave
of desire in her traitorous body.

She never looked back, but headed out to the restaurant,
back to the table where Ronnel was still looking as if he
were about to combust and grabbed her purse.

"I'm ready to go now," she said to him, hoping he'd get
up and they could leave before Jerald could return.

Surely he would have waited until the bathroom was
clear again before coming out. But as soon as Ronnel stood
and she turned to head out of the restaurant, he was there.

He looked as confident and unruffled as he had when
she'd first walked in. His broad shoulders squared, every
handsome feature of his face intact, a stark contrast to how
discombobulated she still felt after their tête-à-tête.

"I'll be in touch," he said in that voice that rubbed seductively over all her exposed nerve endings.

She opened her mouth to speak, to tell him no he wouldn't. She didn't want Ronnel to know that she'd slept with the man that was now his archenemy. How would he react to that? Would he fire her on the grounds of poor judgement? Or would it be as simple as he didn't want her working for him and fucking the man hell bent on taking over his business? Hailey didn't know the answer to any of those questions and her heart beat rapidly as she figured she might be overreacting a bit. But she could not lose this job. Her entire future depended on the income she was receiving from this summer job and she wasn't about to let a man, not even one as good looking and as great in bed as Jerald Carrington interfere with that.

"Do not waste your time," she heard Ronnel say from behind. "I do not have any business with you."

Jerald didn't even blink. "It was a pleasure meeting you, Hailey. Have a good evening."

Had he whispered her name? Did his "have a good evening" sound like he was implying she would have a good evening with him, later or sometime in the future? Hailey took a deep breath, letting it out slowly before finding a small smile and replying, "Thank you. Have a good evening, Mr. Carrington."

Ronnel's gentle hand on her elbow as he guided her out of the restaurant only made Hailey more anxious. Just as when she'd left the ladies' room, she did not turn back to look at Jerald. But she knew he was staring at her, knew he watched every step she took until she was no longer in his line of vision. Her skin heated with that thought, continuing to tingle with an awareness of him, his fingers digging deep inside her, the still dampness of her underwear and fullness of her breasts, as she slid into the backseat of Ronnel's limo.

Hailey sat back against the cool leather seat, staring out the window as they drove through downtown L.A., not breathing easily until the rolling hills of green and the long driveway up to Ronnel's estate came into view.

She was safe here, she thought. Away from Jerald Carrington and his knowing gaze, his hungry kisses and dangerously erotic hands. Yes, Hailey thought, stepping out of the limo and walking toward the house, this was where she belonged—for now. Half an hour away from the city and the man that threatened everything she'd ever wanted and needed in her life.

Ronnel's house was a magnificently conceived Spanish Hacienda with warmth and elegance situated on the crest of Southern California's Palos Verdes Peninsula. Located on the eight acres of land the main residence had nine bedrooms and twenty bathrooms, a tennis court, a gorgeous courtyard featuring Mediterranean herbs, trees and flowers, a guest house, a spacious and bright patio with an infinity pool and breathtaking views of downtown L.A., the San Gabriel Mountains and the white-strand beaches of Santa Monica Bay.

Hailey's favorite place was the pool. She'd always loved to swim, since the summer when she was six years old when her grandfather had taught her. Pops had been patient letting her squeal at water getting into her eyes for the first time, holding her steady while the concept of floating escaped her time and time again. And when she was finally successful, they'd celebrated with him calling Gram out to see her swim in an awkward circle on her own. Later that evening, Gram had fixed her favorite dinner—grilled cheese with bacon and peanut chip brownies for dessert. Those had been the happy times, before Pops became sick.

Every night since she and the girls had come back from the island vacation, she went for a swim before heading up to bed. Tonight, she figured she needed that stress reliever more than ever. She just needed to change into her bathing suit—the new one that she'd bought after trashing the one she'd worn in Turks and Caicos. But the moment she entered her room she frowned at the fact that she was not alone.

"We waited up for you," Malaya said sitting up in the center of Hailey's bed, her shoulder length hair pulled into a high tail that swung along her neck.

"I have something to talk to you about," Rhia added from her spot in the recliner across the room from the bed. The older Mendoza sister left her raven black hair long and hanging almost to her bottom. There were flirty little curls at the ends today and what looked like a fresh coat of make-up highlighting all her great features—smoky dark eyes and those full, pouty lips. Rhia Mendoza was definitely a looker at sixteen. Hailey knew that by the time the girl was an adult, the guys would be knocking down the door to get to her.

"She just wants to talk about boys," Malaya added. "That's all she ever wants to talk about."

Hailey had closed the door, reminding herself that these girls, coupled with their father and his business dealings, were the reasons she was able to stay at this gorgeous estate for the next two months. They were also the reason why in just one more year she'd be able to graduate with a degree in Linguistics, pay off more of the medical bills left by her grandfather and possibly get that job teaching abroad.

"Boys are a very interesting topic," Hailey told them when she'd crossed the room, dropping her purse onto the stand beside her bed and toeing off the four inch sandals she'd worn to the dinner.

She thought of one member of the male gender at that moment that was beyond interesting. He was perplexing and alluring and...

"His name's Brad," Malaya continued in a sing-songy voice as Hailey sat on the bed. "He plays lacrosse."

Rhia looked as if she could strangle her sister at that moment and Hailey chuckled. "Okay, why don't you head

on over to your bedroom and I'll be in there in a few
minutes to tuck you in."

Malaya fake pouted. "I'm too old to be tucked in," she
told Hailey with a toss of her head.

"Well then, I guess we can take that stuffed sheep
you've got on your bed away too, since you're too old."

"No!" Malaya immediately replied, scooting off the bed
and heading for the door. "I don't want to hear this
conversation anyway. *Batang lalaki panganganak*," she
added before sticking her tongue out at Rhia and escaping
before her older sister could give chase.

"She's such a baby," Rhia complained.

Hailey looked at the teenager, still holding her chuckle
over Malaya's signature younger sister behavior. While
she'd been hired to teach these girls English, it had only
take a week away from their father and the confines he put
on them, to realize they—unlike Ronnel—had excellent
command of the language. Upon hiring her, Ronnel, had
told Hailey that the girls had only attended schools in
Bacolod where the family had previously lived. But once
they were at the beach and it was just them and Hailey, the
girls confided that they spoke perfect English because of
the tutor they'd had for the last two years. They'd been
traveling a lot, staying in different places for different
amounts of time so their father had hired a full time tutor to
travel with them. The tutor had taught them to speak and
write English. Ronnel always spoke to his children in
Filipino and he expected them to do the same, saying
English was only required when they were in school or
among the American people. That in their house they
would uphold their heritage.

Hailey had been an only child, her parents having died
in a car accident when she was four years old. Her
grandparents had raised her so there was a certain amount
of solitude that over the years she'd come to both
appreciate and despise. Watching Rhia and Malaya together

had become a private joy for her, one she knew she was going to miss at the end of the summer.

"So, first, let's be clear," Hailey said bunching her dress between her legs as she sat in the center of her bed. "Boys are not boring as your sister just said."

Rhia tilted her head, a sheet of dark, luxurious hair flanking her left shoulder as she did. In a couple of years the girl was going to be simply stunning. Hailey fully expected to be standing in the grocery store one day, picking up a fashion magazine and seeing Rhia's warm brown eyes staring back at her.

"He is American," Rhia immediately confided.

The young girl stood from the chair, coming to sit on the edge of the bed across from Hailey.

"And he's older," she continued on a sigh, sliding to the center of the bed and crossing her legs like Hailey.

Rhia was sixteen. Older could mean two or three years, but Hailey suspected that was off the mark.

"How much older?" she asked wanting to proceed cautiously with this particular conversation.

"A lot. I think." Rhia shrugged. "He called the house and I answered. We spoke for only a few minutes but—"

"But you fell instantly in love with his voice," Hailey said thinking of a certain, smooth as honey, voice that echoed in her mind all too often as well.

"He gave me his name and his number," Rhia continued.

Hailey watched the girl's slim fingers clasp together, then apart as she flattened her palms on her knees.

"Did he ask for your father, Rhia? Is that why he called the house phone?"

"No, actually, he had the wrong number. Then we began talking and I liked him. I think he liked me." Rhia shrugged. "I guess that's why he gave me his number."

Hailey nodded.

"And you want to call him sometime. You want to see him." She was beginning to get a bad feeling about this. After listening to Jerald talk of suspicions that Ronnel was involved in a human trafficking ring, Hailey wondered at just what type of people could be calling or coming here. She also pondered if she should be afraid, if some of what Jerald said may have been true. But no, he was probably just saying all that to close the deal. Ronnel couldn't possibly be a danger to her. Not when he'd hired her to also be there for his daughters.

"I just liked talking to him, that's all," Rhia was saying as she fell back onto the pillows. "Have you ever wanted to do something that you know is wrong, Hailey? I mean, deep down inside you know it's really wrong and yet you want to do it anyway. You want to do it badly."

Hailey only had to think about that question for a moment before the answer was clear. But she did not speak it immediately to Rhia, this very impressionable teenager. She did not scream "hell yes!" in response to her question as she thought again of the man with the voice and the hands, and that tongue. The kiss from earlier still replayed over and over in her mind.

"I think—" Hailey began, still trying to formulate what would be the best way to answer Rhia in her mind.

There was a muted buzzing sound and seconds later Hailey's purse fell from the nightstand. Hailey jumped and leaned over the side of the bed to pick it up. She pulled her phone from the side pouch, sighing as she read the message. It was from Jerald. He was giving her twenty minutes to get to the address he'd typed in or, in his exact words, "I'm coming to get you."

What the hell? Hailey thought with a frown. Who the hell did this guy think he was?

"Is that from a guy?" Rhia asked, leaning over so she too could see the phone's screen.

Hailey immediately tossed the phone back into her purse. "No," she lied. "It's just something I ordered. The company's telling me the package has arrived."

Rhia nodded, using both hands to tuck her hair behind her ears. "And you have to go pick it up. That's cool. We can talk tomorrow I guess. During our lesson time." Rhia grinned then as the girls often did when they referenced the time that Hailey was supposed to be teaching them English. Instead, they usually ended up doing things like shopping online or playing cards for money. Malaya was ahead by three dollars and was quickly becoming a master at Go Fish.

Before Hailey could reply, or tell another lie, she thought with irritation, Rhia had slipped off the bed.

"I'll tuck her in so you can get going. Dad won't like it if you are out too late."

Hailey looked immediately at the sixteen year old who stared at her knowingly. Too knowingly, she frowned.

"Thanks, Rhia," was all she managed to say, watching as the girl left her alone in the room.

Pulling out the cell phone again, Hailey looked at the message.

She wasn't going.

She wasn't going to allow Jerald Carrington to suck her into whatever he wanted from her.

Hadn't she already decided that she could not do that?

But Jerald was...what exactly was he? The man she couldn't keep her hands off, the one that made her ache with desire? Or the distraction that might cost her everything?

Tapping the phone to her forehead and closing her eyes she continued to let thoughts filter through her mind.

Would he actually show up here?

Would he even know where here is?

Of course he would. She remembered the way he'd sat calmly and coolly at that table telling what Hailey felt were some of Ronnel's darkest secrets. If what he'd said were actually true. Maybe she should have done a more thorough background check on the man, she probably could have found out about the allegations against his company as well. But Hailey admitted—at least to herself—that she hadn't bothered to dig that deep. All that had mattered was he did own those companies and he did have the capacity to compensate her for her time.

So that's exactly what she intended to do.

She owed Jerald Carrington nothing. Their night on the island had been mutually beneficial and brief—as evidenced by the way he'd planned to simply walk her to her room and then fly off to where she now knew was L.A. Their new connection was a distant one, or rather one she planned to keep distant. That was something she needed to make very clear to him, now before Ronnel found out that she knew him.

Grabbing her purse she hopped off the bed, hurriedly slipping her feet into her sandals once more before leaving her room. She was going to see Jerald Carrington and she was going to tell him not to contact her again, that what they shared—on the island and in the ladies' room—was done.

It was over.

CHAPTER 3

It started the moment she walked into his penthouse.

She'd taken tentative steps and Jerald had closed and locked the door behind her. When she'd turned, poised to say something he'd simply reacted, moving in, slipping his arms around her waist and taking her mouth in searing hot kiss. The second their tongues collided he could swear he'd seen fireworks go off and for Jerald that was not just a metaphor. Something exploded inside his body and his mind, awakening a hunger that had long lay dormant.

His dick was already hard, his body poised and ready to be reunited with hers once again. His hands roamed up and down, from the rounded globes of her ass, up to the thin straps of her dress that crisscrossed over her back. Her hair was up in some sort of clip, the nape of her neck soft and warm as he cupped a hand there, tilting her head back so that he could kiss her even deeper. He wanted to devour her, right here in the foyer of his condo he wanted to be totally consumed by this woman he thought he'd never see again.

After the first startled seconds she wrapped her arms around his neck, holding him close, diving into that kiss as ferociously as he had. And when he reached down to her ass again, lifting her into his arms, she immediately wrapped her legs around his waist. Jerald began walking, knowing without a doubt where he wanted to take her first tonight. Because in his mind he'd already planned a very long night of exploring every inch of her body, taking the time he hadn't when they were on the island. When she was just an employee of The Corporation.

That thought had him pausing at the first of the steel steps that led up to his bedroom.

"You aren't being paid for tonight," he said pulling his mouth slowly from hers. "This isn't a part of your job assignment."

She looked at him as if she hadn't understood a word he'd said, her eyes glossy, lips swollen from his kiss. Then she pulled her arms back, moving until he released her and her legs straightened, sandal-clad feet clicking as they made contact with the steps.

"I don't work for you," she said finally, brushing her palms down the front of her dress. "As a matter of fact," she continued, pushing past him and stepping down so that she was now more in the living room area than about to go upstairs where he could lay her down on his bed.

"That's what I came here to tell you."

Jerald turned as she proceeded to talk, taking a deep breath in between sentences. Her cheeks were flush. A long strap crossing over her body ending at a box shaped purse nestled on her right side. The strap of the purse separated her breasts—her full, probably somewhere around D or DD cup, breasts—that made his mouth water.

"I work for the man you're trying to destroy. Being here with you right now is likely jeopardizing my job and I cannot afford to let that happen."

She'd started speaking but Jerald had been looking at her body, remembering his hands lifting her dress and finding her pussy hot and wet for him earlier tonight in that bathroom. As such, he hadn't really heard what she'd said. Or at least he thought he hadn't.

"What are you saying?" he asked, feeling his brow furrowing now. His gaze returned to her face just in time to see her tongue take a swipe along her lips before retreating back inside her mouth. His dick twitched as he folded his arms over his chest.

"You're working for Ronnel Mendoza? That's why you were with him tonight?"

"Yes," she said with an exasperated sigh. "I work for him and so I cannot be here with you."

Every muscle in Jerald's body tensed, not with desire, but with irritation this time. He did not want her with anyone else. Not in another man's bed and definitely not letting another man enter her.

She was his.

The thought came quick and shockingly, like a splash of ice cold water and he wasn't sure how to react. He was only certain of one thing.

Jerald took a step towards here.

"You cannot work for him," he said slowly and was deathly serious. "Who is your representative at The Corporation? I'll call them right now and take care of this."

She was already shaking her head, backing away from him. Jerald kept moving toward her.

"Tell me the name and I'll make sure they know you are only to work with me."

Because he couldn't stand the thought of her with someone else. He, the man that had long since decided that there would never be one woman for him, never one person that would accept every dark and eerie part of his past, would never desire a monogamous relationship. He'd also long since gotten over the pain and disappointment of that fact. His parents had a happy and flourishing marriage. And lately, it seemed as if his brothers had also been blessed in that department. Because of one damning night Jerald knew he wouldn't have such a prosperous fate. But that was fine. He'd told himself that a long time ago and he'd meant it. He didn't need love and forever. He only needed the urgency of right now.

And in this moment that urgency was named Hailey.

"The Corporation? I don't know what you're talking about. I work for Mr. Mendoza. I'm a translator for him and his daughters, that's why I was at the meeting tonight. I don't know about any corporation or a representative," she said with a frown.

Then she reached up a hand to tuck away a couple fly-away strands of hair behind her ear.

"What happened in Turks and Caicos, that was absolutely consensual," she began before taking another deep breath and releasing it somewhat hastily. "But it was only one night. Nothing more."

Did she say she didn't work for The Corporation? Jerald had thought she had since she'd been sitting on the beach directly across from the balcony which lead to the ballroom at the resort where they'd been hosting their annual summer celebration. He'd placed an order for the night and told the representative to send the woman he'd hired for the night out to the beach where he'd gone for some fresh air. When he'd seen her sitting there, her legs partially gaped open, the material of her skirt sticking seductively to her thighs, her breasts all but pouring out of her bikini top, he'd assumed she was there for him.

"You're a translator for Mendoza?" he asked by way of clarifying and trying to wrap his mind around the fact that she'd slept with him that night and wasn't on The Corporation's payroll or otherwise beholden to do so.

"Yes," she replied. "That is why I cannot be here with you."

Her words were cut off as he'd moved so close and she'd backed away so many times that finally her back smacked against the beige painted wall. The softness of her breasts pressing into his chest almost made Jerald gasp. He moved in even closer until she was still trying to get away but instead went up on her tiptoes, her eyes widening, and mouth gaping slightly.

"But you *want* to be here with me," he said to her.

Just as she had wanted to be with him that night on the beach. The mere thought had his pulse quickening.

"I...," she hesitated. "I wanted to tell you in person why this couldn't continue."

Jerald traced a finger along her jaw, touching a small mole on the left side of her face.

"It can't? Even though I can tell that's not how you really feel?" he asked her, his gaze holding hers captive. "You want to be here with me, don't you Hailey? You want me to take you again and again."

She started to say something but then stopped, shaking her head slowly.

"I can't," was her eventual reply.

"But you want to," Jerald persisted. "Say it, Hailey. Tell me you want me to take you again."

"I—" she began but stopped when his finger stroked along her lower lip.

It was fuller than the top one, devoid of the gloss he'd seen on them when she'd first walked in. Her brows were perfectly arched, lashes long and feathery.

"Mr. Carrington," she began. "This is not going to work."

"Oh it is, Hailey. It definitely is," he said and instead of waiting for her to respond dipped his head low enough to run his tongue along the rise of cleavage she displayed.

She gasped, her chest rising higher as if she were attempting to feed him more. Jerald took that offer, going further until his tongue was pressing into the crevice that divided her breasts. He moved further until his face was practically buried between her soft mounds.

Hailey clasped the back of his head then and Jerald felt his carefully maintained control shake. It was a mild reaction, but one nonetheless. Moving a knee he pushed her legs apart. She immediately thrust herself upward, like she was more than ready to ride him. Her pussy rubbed seductively along his knee and Jerald lifted it higher, let her press into him further. She was aching, he knew, because

that feeling had been with him every second of every day
since the night at the beach. Magnified by the number of
times he'd watched their video.

"You have to tell me this time," he said, lifting a hand to
reach down the front of her dress gripping her plump
breast.

Pushing the material down simultaneously Jerald pulled
the mound free, instantly flicking his tongue over the
puckered nipple.

"You have to say you want me to take you. I need your
permission," he told her. "Fuck! I need you to say the
words."

Or he was sure he would die, right here, right now, with
his dick harder than it had ever been in his life, and
certainly harder than he'd ever imagined it would be again
after the accident.

Her response was a gasp, her body shivering as he
continued to suckle on her breast. He cupped the other
breast, squeezing hard as her turgid nipple rolled over the
flat of his tongue. Her hands gripped the back of his head
tighter, her hips jutting forward. She was losing the battle
and he was damned glad.

"Yes," she whispered. "Yes!"

It took every ounce of strength Jerald possessed to pull
his mouth away from her tender flesh, but he did. He
cupped his arms beneath her bottom once more and loved
how instantly her legs went around his waist. Taking the
steps two at a time he had them upstairs and entering his
bedroom in seconds. There was only a moment's hesitation
as he stood next to his bed.

There had never been a woman here.

He'd never wanted one to be.

Pushing that thought from his mind he released his hold
on Hailey, loving the feel of her body sliding down his until
she was now on her feet. When she looked up at him Jerald
felt unsteady. It was a quick feeling, just as he'd

experienced moments before. A jolt of something strange that he refused to waste time trying to figure out.

He reached for her dress then, gathering the material in his hands and lifting it up over her head. She'd carried a purse when she came in but he couldn't remember now where it was, not when her breasts were bare and hanging heavily scant inches away from him. He cupped them once more, could not resist palming them and feeling their weight. The action made his body heat and his throat tighten. He yanked his hands away, pushing her panties down past her hips, waiting while she stepped out of them. The sandals she wore were a shade of green he hadn't seen often, the same shade of green as the belt at the waist of her dress. His fingers traced along the straps that wound their way up past her ankles, creating an alluring crisscrossing design along the bronzed tone of her skin. His teeth clenched, mouthwatering as he stared from one foot to the other, aroused in a way that he'd never been before by something as simple as a woman wearing shoes. He continued to touch her, moving down to circle her ankles, down further to brush lightly over the painted tips of her toes. It was then that he saw it, his fingers shaking.

He was nervous.

Again.

Yanking his hands away Jerald moved quickly placing Hailey on the bed—shoes included—before moving to his nightstand. Retrieving a condom he handed the packet to her before stripping his own clothes off tossing them onto the floor instead of putting them into the clothes hamper or the dry cleaners bag as he normally did when he undressed. At this moment, a habit that had come to be more like a ritual for him, became additional seconds that he could not afford to lose with her.

Jerald climbed onto the bed, spreading her legs similar to the way he had that night on the island, but this time he looked down at her, saw the wet folds of her pussy and shook all over. He remembered touching her here, could still hear the sound of her juices stirring at the touch of his fingers. He loved that sound, loved the enticing scent she carried when she was aroused and thought about touching her again. But no, not this time.

This time, Jerald wanted to taste her. He wanted his tongue licking over those plump folds of her flesh, tasting the glistening honey that coated her there. He wanted to delve deep into that oozing center, to feel the tightness that would soon surround his dick gripping his tongue. He wanted to feast on her as if she were a delicacy more distinct than caviar and better tasting than the most famed dessert.

Something else he'd never wanted before.

Another anomaly that he wouldn't waste time trying to consider.

"Put it on," he said in a gruff, impatient voice. "Put it on now."

When Jerald looked to her face he realized that she'd been staring quizzically at him while he'd been contemplating what he knew was an impossibility. He rubbed the inside of her thighs then, massaging them until she was once again sighing, lifting up from the bed to roll the condom down his length. When she pulled her hands away from his thick length Jerald was more than ready to sink inside of her.

But this time, she had other plans.

Hailey remembered their night on the beach as if it were yesterday. She recalled the way he'd looked at her and touched her until she'd shivered, her teeth chattering with her urgent need. She also recollected how he'd taken her so masterfully, so matter-of-factly, being sure to prove what he'd said to her on the beach, that she would enjoy having sex with him.

She had.

And she intended to again, one last time.

But on her own terms.

Flattening her palms on his chest Hailey pushed him back on the bed until the top of his head reached the bed's edge. His body was hard and perfectly sculpted, muscles bulging as if he might have endeavored to be a bodybuilder instead of a businessman. He was glorious, she thought as she straddled him, her legs spreading wider than they ever had before to accomplish this feat.

He stared up at her in question but did not speak, only let his hands fall to her thighs, grasping her skin until she shook. The nipples of his pectorals were dark and flat, slightly puckered and alluring. She wanted to lick him there and along the unmistakably defined board of his abs, but instead she grabbed his thick length once more, loving how it filled her one hand while she aimed it at her waiting center. On a deep inhale she settled herself over him, lowering slowly while her body once again opened and clenched around him.

She sighed. She couldn't help it. Not once since that night at the beach had she felt this aroused and this close to getting the release she so desired. For the last month she'd purchased not one, but two new vibrators. She had plugs and clamps, beads and even floggers in an attempt to bring herself at least a fraction of the intensity she'd felt at his hand. It had all been for nothing as there was just no comparison.

When he thrust upward quickly implanting himself deep inside of her Hailey screamed, then moaned. Steadying herself over him she refocused her mind on taking at least some of the control this time around. She circled her hips, letting him settle inside of her as she stared down into his eyes.

They were hooded, as if he were hiding even though they were as intimately exposed as any two people could be. He was a classically handsome man with intense and attractive eyes. He had a strong jaw and medium thick lips.

Hailey also figured, he was also a man that appreciated good sex, expected it. And she was going to give it to him.

Rising up until he was almost completely out of her she had the distinct pleasure of watching his eyes darken, and a muscle in his jaw twitch before she lowered down on him once more. Then she began to pump in earnest, leaning into him while she drove her hips up and down his shaft.

By way of reaction his hands had grasped her hips, fingers digging deep into her side as he matched her up and down thrusts. With a groan he moved a hand upward pressing her back so that she fell farther forward, her breasts hanging between them. He dipped his head then, taking her nipple into his mouth and sucking deep. She felt like she was being milked and loved every second of it as she continued to slam her pussy down onto him with every bit of strength she had.

She heard herself gasping for air, moaning and whispering how good it felt. Her body trembled over his, eyes closing then struggling to open again. All the while his facial features remained strained, as if he were holding back any more of a reaction than the hardness of his cock slamming into her.

Hailey was not pleased and she pulled up and off him quickly, thinking maybe this had been a mistake after all. Sex had not been her original purpose for coming here tonight.

But the minute she'd arrived he'd touched her and kissed her and...she'd lost all that conviction. She'd decided on one more time and then that would be it. Only now, she was realizing that may have been a mistake. Jerald hadn't been at all concerned with what she'd had to say. And even now as they were having sex—what she'd thought he'd wanted all along—he was still acting as if there were something else he'd rather be doing.

Maybe he was one of those guys that could only get off on control. She'd read about them in the sexy books she borrowed from the library when she grew tired of studying.

He was always giving her commands instead of asking if she'd like to do anything, always assuming that what he needed and wanted was the only thing that mattered.

Hailey was positive that wasn't a situation she could deal with. No matter how good the end result was. She wanted that blissful orgasm, wanted it enough to put aside her real reason for coming here to get it. But in the end, she figured it wasn't worth his lack of interest and the looming possibility that this night might end just as embarrassingly for her as it had on that island.

Hailey was on her knees about to climb off the bed when he moved quickly, grabbing her by the waist as he came up behind her. His dick was slipping down the crevice of her ass, easing ever so easily into her pussy once more. And then it really began.

The pounding of her heart as his dick moved in and out of her with speed and succinct aim, rubbing against every erogenous spot she figured she possessed. He held her hips still as he moved, his breath coming in steady pants. Her fingers clenched the sheets as she bit into her bottom lip, his pumping felt so damned good. He was so deep inside of her she felt like they may now be connected on more than just a physical level—like he was actually a part of her. And all thoughts of leaving vanished from her mind.

"Jerald," she whispered, trying it out. It sounded right echoing throughout the room and Hailey said it again and again.

"Yes," he replied to her surprise. "It's me, Hailey. It's all me."

And that was no lie, Hailey thought as he slammed into her one more time and the damn finally broke. Her body shook, her arms almost giving out on her. She closed her eyes as her release rippled through her like a torrential storm. Gritting her teeth was the only thing that kept her from yelling out with the immense pleasure she felt. He pulled out of her then, even as her body continued to convulse, flipping her over and onto her back.

Jerald lifted her legs up onto his shoulders, then thrust into her again. He cupped her breasts this time as he worked himself in and out of her with quick deep thrusts. Through the haze of euphoria she was feeling Hailey managed to look up at him, to see how intently he stared down at her. His brow was furrowed, his lips drawn in a straight line almost as if he were somehow angry. But his moans told another story. Was he actually enjoying this?

At that moment he tensed and she could feel his dick pulsating inside of her, his release emptying into the condom while his hands still gripped her tightly.

Hailey reached up then, rubbing her hands along his chest, touching his pectorals and then his biceps. She sighed his name again, only to have him stiffen. He let her legs down gently and slipped from the bed, just like he'd done that night on the island.

Only this time, Hailey was faster.

"Is this your MO?" she asked, now mildly annoyed at the moist remnants of her release along her inner thighs.

She crossed her legs then reached for the sheet, pulling it around her body.

"You can't keep your hands off a woman, bringing her to the brink of coming as she stands in front of you. Then you get her into bed, screw her brains out and walk away? Is that what Jerald Carrington does on a regular basis?"

Her words stopped him cold, his broad back and deliciously taut ass on full display.

"You wanted me too," he said tightly. "You told me so."

"I won't deny that," Hailey admitted. "But I didn't ask for the cold shoulder afterwards."

"There is nothing else to give," he told her, still without turning to face her.

Hailey knew he was right. Controlled and distant. That was the type of man he was. She didn't think she liked it, then realized that it really didn't matter.

"You're absolutely correct, there is nothing else," she said with resignation. "But this time I'm showering first and then I'm leaving."

She was off the bed then, circling around the spot where he stood still as a statue until she was right in his face. She grasped the sheet even tighter because dammit, his dick was still hard and her nipples had immediately reacted to the sight.

"I'm leaving and we're never doing this again. I won't let you mess up my future, regardless of how good the sex is." She hadn't meant to say that last part but since she hadn't managed to do or say anything the way she'd planned tonight, Hailey simply shrugged and let the statement go.

He didn't say anything, just gave her that same serious, here-but-not-really-giving-a-damn look. It was the perfect look for him, matching seamlessly with the man she'd seen earlier, the aloof and arrogant businessman not at all used to losing. He was a shark, a predator, always going in for the kill. As for her, Hailey knew there was no competition here. She was not on Jerald Carrington's level and a big part of her was glad for that fact. Her goals in life were to help people, to travel the world and see and enjoy as much as she could while learning even more about her trade.

Getting involved with Jerald Carrington—or rather sleeping with him—was not in the plan.

With that thought, Hailey turned from him and headed for the bathroom, slamming the door behind her. There was a lock on the door for which she would be forever grateful and she slipped it into place, leaning aback against it to let out the deep breath she'd just taken.

She was the stranger here, she reminded herself. The fish out of water, might be a more accurate description. And if Jerald were the predator she was in danger the longer she stayed. Be that as it may, there was a distant part of her that wanted to sob with sadness that this really gorgeous guy who seemed so in tuned to her every physical need was not "The One", the way her grandmother had sworn her grandfather had been "The One" for her. No, Hailey thought with a quick shake of her head. This was the real world and she was dealing with real life obstacles— financial ones that haunted her each time she closed her eyes. There was no room for fantasies or hopelessly romantic premonitions. None whatsoever and the more she kept that fact in mind, the better off she would be.

THE ONE

He insisted on following her home. His tone unyielding no matter how much she argued. And she did argue, back and forth, for several minutes, telling him it was unnecessary.

I agreed.

But he didn't.

And so Jerald followed Hailey home. The engine in the Agate Pearl colored Lexus Fire that he drove quietly starting, as he pulled out of the parking garage right behind the Mercedes SUV she was driving.

I pulled out behind him, following at a safe distance as they drove through the city and out toward the cliffs. The sound of my voice counting to twenty, pausing and then starting over again echoed throughout the interior of my vehicle. I didn't want music right now. There was no song, no lyrics, and no instruments that could calm me. Only simple breathing could tackle that task. And so I breathed and counted and counted and breathed, and drove behind those two like some fanatical stalker in the middle of the night.

This wasn't how this was supposed to go. It's not what I had planned. And yet, here I was, doing the unthinkable and hating every fucking minute of it.

When Jerald stopped at the bottom of the hill and got out, I let my car idle just at the turn in case he looked back. He wouldn't see me. I doubted he'd even be looking at anyone but her. That's how it appeared earlier tonight at Perch. He'd been talking business, but he'd been watching her.

He went to her car, leaned down to the window. They exchanged words that I couldn't hear. Words I didn't want to hear.

She pulled off quickly, leaving him standing there to stare after her car. Then he finally walked back to his vehicle, climbing in the driver's side and turning around. I got out quickly, popping my hood and began looking under it wondering if he'd stop to help.

He did not and I smiled, knowing that one day…one day very soon, I wouldn't be the one that needed help.

They would.

CHAPTER 4

"You need a woman," Lydia Carrington spoke candidly to her middle son. "Someone to show you that there is more to this life than just working all the time. I'd think you never left this office if I didn't see you at the house for Sunday brunch every week."

Jerald was leaning back in his dark leather office chair. It had been all of five minutes since his mother had appeared in the doorway, unannounced. Not that she needed to schedule a time to visit him, but yeah, he would have liked to have been more prepared for this meeting. Still, he was not surprised by her words. She'd been saying as much to him—albeit with more subtlety—since Jackson had announced he was going to marry Tara. To his mother's way of thinking that meant two down and one more to go. Only, the one more, had no intention of going down the marriage road. None whatsoever.

"I'm just fine the way I am, mother," he replied, keeping his tone level so as not to rile her.

Lydia Carrington, while described in both fashion and fortune magazines as an intelligent and well-spoken woman who was the epitome of graceful and demure success, would cut a person off at the knees if she thought they were disrespecting her in any way. As Jerald was her son, she'd likely only give him that searing look she dished out just before the heated words, and if all of the above were not heeded, the quick whack on the back of his head.

"Don't patronize me, Jerald. I am not one of your employees. I do not have to accept that answer you give and go on my merry way."

So his level tone hadn't worked as well as he'd desired. He sat up straighter in his chair, letting his hands—nails perfectly manicured because dirty or uneven nails were yet another pet peeve of his—resting on the arms of the chair.

"That's not what I'm trying to do at all, mother. I just know how this conversation goes and before you waste your time I want to assure you that I am fine. I am happy just the way I am."

Lydia, still a very attractive woman at fifty-seven years old, lifted a perfectly arched brow. Her lips were painted a pretty peach color, tilted upward at the ends—the I-don't-believe-a-word-you're-saying look.

"I'm sure you believe that, Jerald. But I am your mother and I know better."

Jerald sighed then, because he had lost count of how many times he'd heard her say those very words before.

"Why can't a man be content living his life and pursuing his career? I'm not breaking any laws, nor am I planning a world takeover."

"No," she said stopping him before he could say another word. "You're wasting all that I know is inside of you."

That silenced him. Nobody knew what was inside Jerald. They never had.

"It was an accident, Jerald. You were doing something you loved to do, enjoying yourself and an accident happened. It was a hard time after that, a hard and painful one for you, I know. But it passed. You healed and you've been better for just about sixteen years now. At least you've been physically healed," she finished.

There was so much he could say to that, so much he could tell the only woman he'd ever loved about her rendition of the skiing accident that had taken place when he was nineteen years old. But he remained silent, just as he had all these years.

"When is the last time you've been out on a date?" she asked after a few moments of silence.

"I don't date women," he replied curtly.

"Do you date men?" was her follow-up.

He frowned. "No, mother. I do not date men either."

She nodded as if she'd already known that. "And you think that's normal?"

Jerald refused to get angry. He knew his mother was only speaking from the heart. She wanted for him what she had with his father and Jackson and Jason had with their wives. But that would never be. He didn't know how to make her understand that.

"Tell me, Jerald, have you never met a woman that made your heart beat faster? That changed the way you looked at life? When she talks, you listen, intently, as if every word she speaks means something special, something life-altering to you. And when you're with her, you feel so free, so relaxed and at peace that the moment she's away from you there's a sense of loss that takes your breath away. Have you ever felt that Jerald?"

No. His mind screamed with the answer but his lips did not move, no sound could break free. Which was silly because the answer was simple. No, he had never experienced any of those things his mother had mentioned. The only thing Jerald had ever managed to feel for a woman was the tell-tale twitching in his pants. The budding growth of desire as his limp dick slowly came to life, proving that after the spinal cord injury, the temporary paralysis and all that painstaking rehab and physical therapy, that he had in fact healed. For an entire year that stirring and desire had been absent from Jerald's life and it had almost torn him apart. What kind of man would he be if he'd never have another arousal? If he couldn't be with a woman?

Pain had begun to shoot up his arms as Jerald had been clenching his fists so tightly, his temples throbbing as he scolded himself for thinking about such a thing with his mother sitting less than ten feet away from him.

"I do not need to date," he said slowly, through clenched teeth. "What I need to do is close this deal before Jackson gets back from his honeymoon. That is all I need to do, mother. I wish you would please try to understand that."

Lydia stood from her seat, walking purposely until she was on the other side of the desk. She leaned in, cupping her son's chin in her palm and tilting his head up so that she could look into his eyes.

"There's a love out there for you, Jerald. There's healing for that scar you've not only carried on your back but in your heart for whatever reason. You'll find it if you just open your eyes."

He wanted to deny her words again, to ask her to please go away because she would never understand. But Jerald couldn't do it. He loved his mother and he knew she meant well. So he simply sighed and stood from his seat. He took the hand that was on his face, bringing it back to his lips for a kiss before pulling her into a hug.

"I love you, mother," he whispered as he held her close. "Isn't it enough that I love one woman in my lifetime?"

Lydia hugged him tightly, her palms flat on his back, patting him before she pulled back to look into his eyes once more.

"I love you too, son. But no, it's not enough for you to love me. There's room in your heart for another. I know there is."

When Jerald opened his mouth to reply Lydia placed a hand softly over it, shaking her head from side to side.

"We won't speak of it anymore today. You've got to get home and get dressed for the Renquist party. It's at eight and if we're not all there Julianne Renquist will lose what's left of her mind. You know how she likes to show off," she told him.

Jerald managed a smile as he took his mother's hand from his mouth and moved to walk her to the door. His calendar notification had warned him of the party the moment he picked up his cell phone this morning. It was the last place he wanted to be, in a room full of people acting as if he gave a damn about what they had to say or who they wanted him to meet.

He'd much rather be at home watching his video. The new one starring Hailey. The one he'd recorded a week ago when he'd last seen her.

"I'll be there," he told his mother. "I won't like it, but I'll be there."

"Nobody will like it, darling," Lydia said with a chuckle before kissing him on the cheek and walking out of his office.

Hailey hated this dress.

From the emerald green color that she thought was too dark for a humid summer evening, to the boxed neckline in the front to the plunging back that almost reached the crack of her butt. Her breasts were too big to go unbound, her waist, not nearly skinny enough to pull off the sexy svelte look she figured this dress should display. The best part of the outfit were the shoes, Gianvito Rossi was the name on the box, five inch heels, embellished ankle strap sandals. She loved how they sparkled and made her feel almost like Cinderella.

There was a black box on the bed. It had been sitting there when she'd returned from her swim this afternoon, along with the garment bag that contained this dress. The instructions on the slip of paper with Ronnel's initials at the top were simple: Be ready at seven. Hailey had raced to her phone and pulled up her calendar thinking she couldn't possibly have forgotten about some meeting Ronnel had. He'd had them all week long with men discussing investing in his company. None of them had been committal, however, and by the time the meeting was over Hailey had begun to feel like maybe Jerald had been right—high-handed, inconsiderate and arrogant as hell—but right nonetheless. Ronnel's only option to save face may very well lie with Carrington Enterprises.

Despite the inner warnings, Hailey had done some research on that particular company, learning of the three Carrington brothers, two of which ran the acquisitions company with sophisticated superiority. They were good looking men, including the father, Jeffrey. And their mother was beautiful, the elegant kind of woman that made you think of old money and big houses. None of which Hailey had ever had.

There had been no meeting on her calendar for Ronnel tonight that was why she'd taken a leisurely afternoon sightseeing with Rhia and Malaya. When they'd returned she'd gone for a late swim. Tonight she'd planned to catch up on some reading, anything to keep her mind off Jerald Carrington. Well, she thought with a sigh, she'd definitely be able to do that since it seemed she'd be spending her Friday night translating another business meeting and avoiding the quizzical glare Ronnel had begun giving her.

She walked to the bed and was about to pick up the box so she could finish getting dressed. Ronnel did not like to be kept waiting. Her phone rang just as she was about to reach for the box and with a sigh Hailey turned her attention to the small beaded purse that had also been on the bed when she came in. She'd already packed it with the essentials—her tube of lip gloss, a pack of spearmint gum and her cell phone. The keys to Ronnel's SUV, the one he allowed her to drive, were already hanging on the key holder in the kitchen. That's where she'd been instructed to leave them anytime she wasn't driving the girls around. A new rule, which had been announced the morning after she'd come from Jerald's house.

"Hi Gram," Hailey said after looking at the screen of her phone and accepting the call.

"Hi Jellybean," Katherine Jefferson replied, her familiar voice sounding hoarse. Still, Hailey had smiled at the sound of the nickname her grandfather had given her. Only after his death, did her grandmother start calling her the same thing.

"It's so good to hear from you," Hailey replied. She'd been about to sit on the bed then thought better of that idea. She didn't want to wrinkle the ugly dress, so instead she walked across the floor, holding the phone to her ear as she looked around. "I was going to call you in the morning. I know how you enjoy our early morning talks while you're having your coffee."

Every Saturday morning at seven since the first time she'd left home to go to school Hailey had called her grandmother. Katherine would tell her all about her week and then Hailey would do the same. It had felt as if they'd never been apart and made both of the women feel better about the distance that had to be between them for Hailey to succeed.

That, and the hesitation in Katherine's voice alerted Hailey to the fact that something was wrong.

"I know, but I have to tell you something and I couldn't lay down tonight and close my eyes without you knowing," she said.

Hailey licked her lips nervously, not giving a damn about the lip gloss she'd already applied. "What is it, Gram? What's wrong?"

"It's back," her grandmother said simply. "Dr. Carter said it was a possibility last year and I guess now it's a reality. The cancer is back."

Hailey closed her eyes. The hand that had been resting leisurely at her side reaching out to grab the edge of the desk she'd been standing next to.

"He's sure?" Hailey asked knowing the moment it was out what her grandmother would say.

"He's the doctor, dear," she replied.

"We can get a second opinion. Remember the last time we did that they told us something different," Hailey continued, desperation clear in her tone.

"But I still had to undergo surgery to remove the tumors. They found two more this time. Dr. Carter wants to do a biopsy but I know its cancer."

"Gram, you just said it yourself, he's the doctor. You have no way of knowing what's going on inside your body," Hailey tried to reason with her grandmother. She also tried to deny what she'd feared most when she'd left Maitlin to take this job.

"I know what I feel, Jellybean. I get up in the morning and I cough and cough until I feel like I'm going to pass out. Then my chest hurts so bad I can't do anything but lay in bed for hours. I knew it was there even before they saw it on those fancy tests."

The more her grandmother talked, the better Hailey could hear it. The same raspy tone of voice her grandfather had just before he'd been diagnosed with mesothelioma. Her heart beat wildly and so loud it almost drowned out her grandmother's words. This could not be happening again. Fate seemed to hate Hailey with some sort of vengeance.

"When is the biopsy scheduled?" she asked, trying like hell to remain calm.

"Two weeks from Monday. I told Dr. Carter's nurse to call you to make all those other appointments. I'm just so tired and I can't remember everything all the time. That lawyer's office called me the other day too, wanted me to schedule an appointment with their doctors for the asbestos tests. I didn't call them back, didn't really know what to say," she finished with a heavy sigh.

If Hailey closed her eyes again she would see her grandmother sitting in her rocking chair in front of the fireplace in the living room. There were two chairs there, one that had been for Pops and the other for Gram. They used to sit there every evening after dinner while Hailey lay on the rug between them coloring in her books or reading them a story. They loved when she read to them.

"Don't worry, Gram. I'll call Dr. Carter and I'll call the lawyers. I'll handle everything," she promised her.

Hailey always promised the same thing and she did whatever she could to keep that promise. After hanging up with her grandmother she typed an alert on her phone for first thing Monday morning. She would call the doctor's office and find out exactly what was going on with her grandmother and then she would call the lawyers that had sued for wrongful death on Pop's behalf. Ten years ago her grandfather had gone to a lawyer because some of his co-workers had suggested he do so. Apparently, as Pops had made his living working for a steel company down at the docks, he'd unknowingly been exposed to asbestos fibers in some of the materials they'd been using. Residue from those fibers had been embedded in his lungs. Two weeks later the lawyers' office called and suggested Pops see an oncologist. He did and within a month he was diagnosed with mesothelioma, a type of cancer that can only come from exposure to asbestos. It is also incurable.

Squeezing the phone in her hand Hailey tried like hell not to cry. Pops didn't like tears. He said they were unproductive. And Hailey believed him. She had loved him with every ounce of her being and had lost him, just as she feared she was about to lose her grandmother.

The loud knocking on her door had her jumping and she turned just in time to see Ronnel stepping inside her room.

"It is seven," he said stiffly.

Hailey nodded. "Right. I apologize. I just had to deal with this family thing. I'll be down in a second," she told him.

He did not leave right away, but stood there staring at her. The morning after she'd been with Jerald, Ronnel had come into the kitchen during breakfast. He never had breakfast with her and the girls. She had stood to leave believing he wanted to spend time with his daughters, but he'd told her to sit. Throughout the meal each time she'd looked up, Ronnel had been staring at her. It seemed strange, but not as strange as she figured this job

opportunity might look to some. So she'd shrugged it off
and moved on.

Tonight, the look unnerved her. Or maybe that was
because she was still reeling from her grandmother's news.
Whatever it was, this job was now more important than
ever. The money the lawyers were able to recover from the
asbestos manufacturers came slowly and unpredictably. It
usually paid a bit towards the balance of some of the larger
bills but never enough to meet their financial needs. Now,
if her grandmother was indeed sick, they would incur even
more debt. Doctor's visits, surgery, medications and with a
pang of sorrow resting heavily in the center of her chest,
she thought, possibly hospice. And there was still the
promise she'd made to her grandfather that she would be
the first in their family to graduate from college. No, there
was no doubt, Hailey needed this money, now more than
she ever had.

She moved to the bed slipping her phone in the purse,
hearing Ronnel move from the doorway as she did. Hailey
put on the shimmering jewelry that had been incased in that
black box and she slapped more lip gloss on her lips. She
was out the door in less than five minutes, walking down
the marble steps, across the foyer floor and outside to the
waiting limousine. Whatever Ronnel had going on tonight
she would be there. She would smile the way he'd told her
to and translate whatever he needed. Then she would come
back to this house that sometimes seemed more like a
fortress, go to sleep, wake up in the morning and do it all
over again.

Because for Hailey, there was no other choice.

Leonard Renquist was one of the top ten highest paid
Hollywood producers. His wife Julianne had acted in one
of his first movies, almost a million years ago, Jerald
thought with a sigh after he'd made the rounds saying hello
to everyone he needed to. He'd quickly found himself a

corner to hide out in and now sipped his vodka tonic while watching tonight's entertainment.

Retired from acting, Julianne now spent the majority of her time throwing lavish parties citing one worthy cause or another. Jerald couldn't even remember which cause this year's event was for because he figured the "cause" thing was a huge sham anyway. Unfortunately, this was one of the few events his parents were adamant about him and his brothers attending. His mother and Julianne had attended the same private high school and had kept close contact with each other over the years.

"In this world you don't run across true friends often," Lydia had told him one year when he'd complained about attending this event. "Julianne has a good heart so I excuse the fact that all of Leonard's money has her mind filled with fluff."

Jerald smiled as he looked across the room to see Julianne tossing her head back, frosted blonde hair hanging limply past the her shoulders, while her tucked and plucked face attempted what she probably thought was a smile. Her laugh was loud, like a broken horn and the people standing close to her frowned, then tried not to show how irritated by the sound they really were.

It was the same old scene, Jerald thought taking another sip from his glass. He looked at his watch—one hour and fifteen minutes to go. Two hours, that was the respectable amount of time to stay at the party. He, Jackson and Jason had come to that conclusion years ago.

Speaking of which, Jerald came to his feet as Jason and his lovely wife, Celise, approached. They were a breathtaking couple, Jerald admitted to himself. Over the last two and a half years that they'd been together he'd watched them both carefully, seeing how they grew deeper in love with each other every day. In addition, as Jason's Carrington Resorts and Celise's Chances restaurants both began to grow in locations and popularity, Jerald had seen his brother and sister-in-law, not only at family dinners but also on the cover of magazines and doing television interviews. They were an up and coming power couple and looked every inch the part.

Jason wore a dark suit, single breasted and fit to his tall, toned frame. His shirt was also black, his tie a bold and bright pink which precisely matched the color of Celise's fitted gown with the slit up her right leg. Her long, dark hair which she always wore bone straight was pulled to hang seductively over her right shoulder, her smile bright and genuine as she came closer to hug Jerald.

"Hey there. It's good to see you out and about," she said as she pulled away from the embrace.

Jerald didn't ruffle at the reply because his family was always talking about him working too much and/or staying to himself too much. Being the person they'd always known him to be didn't seem to score him any brownie points these days.

"You look stunning," he replied instead, kissing her cheek before moving to shake his brother's hand.

"What do you think if you keep your hair almost bald I wouldn't see the grays beginning to sneak in," Jason, who was the youngest of the Carrington brothers, said rubbing a hand over Jerald's head before pulling his brother into a hug.

Jerald only shrugged. "Aging's a part of life," he told them and finished off his drink.

Timely as ever a member of the staff was walking by with a tray full of champagne. Jerald snagged a flute and put his empty glass on the tray before Jason and Celise were served.

"Right, your birthday's coming up in a couple of months," Celise said from where she stood beside her husband. "The big thirty-five. We should do something grand to celebrate."

Jason nodded. "She's right. You can come on down to Monterey and we'll throw you a huge birthday bash at the hotel."

"Oh yes!" Celise squealed. "I just hired a fabulous pastry chef. He makes the most divine desserts and candy is his specialty. What about a candy sculpture of you to mark the centerpiece of the party?"

"What about nothing," Jerald replied with a frown. "I'll celebrate the same way I have all the years before."

"And how's that? A microwave meal and the remote control while you sit in your room and watch television? Great celebration, big brother." Jason said with a frown.

Jerald only nodded. "It works for me."

"Well not for me," Celise added. "I'm going to speak with your mother about this."

"Wow, aren't we a bit old for you to go running to my mother just because I won't do what you want?" he asked with a slight chuckle, even though a part of him was extremely serious.

"Who plans to go running to me and about what?" Lydia asked coming up behind Jerald placing a hand on his shoulder.

Great, he thought, the gang's all here. Resigning himself to the inevitable Jerald leaned in to kiss his mother's cheek, while Jeffrey Carrington also joined his family. His father kissed Celise and shook Jason's hand before extending his arm to Jerald, who shook his hand dutifully.

"Good to see you, dad," he said thinking that maybe he'd have someone on his side.

Jeffrey had always been the one to stop the barrage of questions and recommendations when they were being hammered towards Jerald. Later he'd clap his middle son on the shoulder and tell him that the Carrington men had to stick together. It had made Jerald feel as if he had someone on his side. Not that he didn't think his family loved and cared about him, it was just that their love and caring could be a bit overwhelming from time to time.

"I was just saying that we should give Jerald a huge birthday party in Monterey this year," Celise jumped right in.

Lydia's smile spread all too fast. "That's a marvelous idea. We could all come down. Jackson and Tara will be all settled by then so they'll come too. We could invite everyone."

"Not everyone," Jason said lifting his brows as he glanced at Jerald. "Just a couple hundred guests. Nothing too splashy. Right, big brother?"

Jason was getting a kick out of this Jerald knew and he wanted to punch him for it. But he didn't and he didn't bother to argue anymore. His father had only nodded as Lydia and Celise continued to talk so Jerald knew he wouldn't be getting any help from him either. These husbands were apparently so besotted with their wives that they would go along with whatever the women said. Pity, Jerald thought with a shake of his head.

Then he stopped.

The chatter of his mother and sister-in-law grew to a dull murmur, the stem of the champagne flute he was holding grew slick between his fingers as his gaze zeroed in on the two people that had just entered the party.

Hailey.

She looked like sex walking in a dress that hugged every curve of her body, flaring out at the bottom to swirl in a puddle of silk on the floor. Diamonds sparkled at her ears and the thick bracelet on her wrist. A gift from Mendoza no doubt.

He grit his teeth, hand clenching that glass so hard it was a wonder it didn't break. Jerald excused himself and was walked away from the group of Carringtons before any of them could stop him.

What was he doing?

She'd made it perfectly clear that she did not want to see him again. During the week since then, Jerald had checked with The Corporation, confirming that Hailey Jefferson was not in their employ. Over the past couple of days he'd had a chance to digest the fact that he'd slept with a woman he'd met on the beach. She hadn't been vetted through The

Corporation, tested for any diseases and her background run through a government level check. And yet, the moment he'd had another chance, he'd slept with her again.

But there was one thing Jerald prided himself on—even though he was seriously beginning to doubt his abilities where this woman was concerned—he did not beg. Hailey had said she did not want to see him again. She hadn't texted or called him in seven days. He took that seriously and had left her alone.

And now she was here.

On his turf, Jerald thought as he stood just a few feet away from her now. She was smiling and greeting everyone who came up to Mendoza. It was no shock that the billionaire knew a lot of the people here. He was in the fashion industry, even though the company specialized in lower end department store garments. The new accessories line he'd launched a couple months ago, however, had been the feature of all the Fashion Weeks and his name had been quietly circulating. Unfortunately, that was probably too little, too late, to save his company.

Jerald wanted to approach her. No, he actually wanted to take her by the hand and lead her upstairs to one of the rooms. From the side her breasts and ass made a tempting silhouette. When she leaned in close to hug a woman who insisted, Jerald saw all the bronzed skin of her back and his mouth watered. His dick hardened and he knew.

He would have her again.

Mendoza was in deep conversation with two gentlemen when Jerald moved up to stand behind Hailey. He leaned in slightly to whisper, "Come with me."

She startled, he could tell by the quick stiffening of her shoulders. But she did not turn around. She knew it was him.

The air around him hummed with sexual tension. Jerald could feel it like a warm breeze over his skin. He'd already walked away from her but he knew she would follow him.

His heart had begun a steady rapid rhythm his hands clenching at his sides.

What was he doing? The question resonated in his mind again and again. She said she didn't want to see him and yet he'd gone to her and beckoned her. Would she really come? He didn't doubt it although a part of him said he should have. He wasn't paying her, she had no reason to come to him. No reason to want him the way he found himself wanting her. But, she did.

When Jerald stopped in one of the farthest corners of the room, near the windows overlooking the city, he turned his back from that gorgeous view, only to feel his body continue to heat as his gaze once again rested on her.

She looked far better than the lighted tips of the L.A. skyscape. With her hair pulled back tightly into a bun that sat at an alluring angle to the side of her head she looked regal and sophisticated. That dress, the deep jewel-tone color and the simple, yet strikingly enticing design, had him gulping before he could speak.

"What are you doing here?" he asked her.

She clenched the beaded purse she was holding in front of her with both hands.

"Working, I presume," was her response.

"I thought you only needed to translate for his business meetings."

"I did too," she replied. "That's what our deal was. Today, however, he gave me all this and told me to be ready. So here I am."

"At his beck and call," Jerald replied sarcastically.

Hailey shook her head. "On his payroll."

He took a step closer to her as if those words had lit the flame inside of him. "I have much more money than he does. He's about to lose everything."

One elegantly arched brow lifted in question. "Are you offering me a job?"

Jerald did not reply. He was asking her for something. He knew that as surely as he knew his name. Only he had no idea what.

"Hello there."

Jerald frowned at the sound of his mother's voice. Hailey, to her credit, turned immediately, smile already in place.

"Hello," she said, extending her hand the way she had been doing with those that had come up to greet Mendoza. "I'm Hailey Jefferson."

Lydia smiled as well, taking the younger woman's hand. "I'm Lydia Carrington, Jerald's mother. You're delightfully pretty, Ms. Jefferson."

Jerald slipped a hand into his pocket adjusting the bulging erection that pressed painfully against the zipper of his slacks. He looked at Hailey as his dick throbbed again. Even her blush was sexy as hell.

"Thank you," she said to Lydia.

"I hope my son is being a gentleman," Lydia continued.

"I suspect he's being his usual self," Hailey replied lightly.

Lydia chuckled. "Are you new in town, Hailey? I haven't seen you at this party before."

And Lydia would have seen a woman like Hailey around town, Jerald thought. She would not quickly be forgotten, not with her fresh and unmarred look. The naturally tanned tone of her skin and those high cheekbones that gave her face an exotic flare. There was more than Jerald could not forget about this woman, more than was running rampantly through his mind at this very moment.

"No ma'am, I'm from Virginia. I'm just here for the summer," Hailey told her.

Lydia nodded. "Oh really? Vacation then?"

"I wish," Hailey chuckled. "I'm working here this summer and heading back east in the fall for my final year in college."

"A college student," Lydia continued with a glimpse over to her son. "How old are you, my dear?"

Jerald was uncomfortable. Not at his mother's friendly interrogation of Hailey because he'd been lucky all his life not to have had her questioning any female he'd spent time with. But he wanted to touch Hailey, to kiss her and feel the weight of her breasts—her unbound breasts by the sight of her puckered nipples pressing tastily through the material of her dress—in the palm of his hands.

The fact that his mother was standing right there while he lusted after this woman was what made him extremely uncomfortable and he silently wished for something to happen to change the situation.

"I'm twenty-five and I'm working my way through school. I will finish in the next year."

This time Hailey's voice had a slight edge, as if she were trying to convince not only his mother, but herself of this fact.

She cleared her throat then. "Ah, I should get back. If you'll excuse me. It was very nice to meet you Mrs. Carrington."

All of that was spoken in a matter of seconds and then she was walking away, the plump globes of her ass moving sinuously in that damned gown.

"A little young for you, don't you think?" Lydia said when she was alone with her son.

"It's not what you think," Jerald said tightly.

"Right," was his mother's reply. "But she is gorgeous."

Yes, he thought, she is.

"I'll be right back," Jerald said without waiting for another of his mother's replies.

He was moving quickly, pushing past people trying to get to Hailey before she could meet up with Mendoza again. He grabbed her arm just before she turned a corner.

"What are you doing?"

"We're not finished," he told her, continuing to move until they were out of the room and near the bank of elevators.

He slapped his palm against the button and turned back to her.

"Jerald," she said with a sigh. "I already told you—"

"And yet you came," he said stepping closer to her, so close her nipples rubbed alluringly against his chest. "When I called, you came. Your nipples are so hard right now I can feel them," he continued, taking a quick swallow. "Dammit Hailey, I can remember how they taste. I remember how you smell, how your pussy feels clenching around my dick. Tell me you don't remember that. Tell me you don't want to feel it again. Do it. I dare you."

The door to the elevator opened and she continued to stare at him. Her breathing had increased, he could see the rapid pulse beat in her neck. She kept her mouth shut, her hands fisted at her sides and he knew she was trying. She was reaching for the strength to deny him. He could have told her that attempt was futile.

Jerald pulled her into the elevator and pressed the button to hurry and close the door. Once it was closed he was on her, pressing her against the wall of the compartment, crashing his lips down over hers immediately.

She kissed him back. Just like that. No resistance and no argument. He groaned with the knowledge, grinding his hips against her so that she could feel his arousal.

"I don't know why," she whispered when he pulled his mouth away and kissed along her jaw. He loved the taste of her skin right there. "I can't figure it out."

Jerald shook his head.

"Me either," he was saying, his hands gripping her ass.

Hailey pushed an arm between their bodies, cupping his dick in her palm, squeezing, then rubbing before squeezing again.

Jerald sucked in a breath feeling as if he might come right at this very moment.

"I want to be inside you," he told her. "I want to fuck you right here, right now."

To solidify his comment Jerald reached over to the control panel, pressing a button that immediately stopped the elevator.

Hailey gasped, letting her head fall back against the wall. "No," she told him. "I can't. Not here. He'll know I'm gone."

She was talking but Jerald was already pulling on the material of her dress, pushing it upward until his hands scrapped along the bare skin of her thigh.

"I don't care," he told her, taking her mouth again.

His tongue delved deep, tangling with hers as she tilted her head to the side. She sucked his tongue into her mouth and Jerald cupped the V of her juncture, hating the wisp of lace that was acting like a barrier between him and ecstasy.

"Jerald," she sighed when the sexy as hell kiss was over. "Please."

"I am baby," he replied. "I am."

His fingers moved the lace aside and he pressed quickly into her, two fingers going deep into her already wet center. He watched as she bit her bottom lip and began to pump against his hand.

"Stop," she whispered, her eyes closed. "Please stop."

It was the barest of whispers and for a second Jerald continued to pump inside of her loving the heat and warmth surrounding his fingers, the dampness he wanted to lick free.

"Jerald," she continued on a ragged breath. "I want you to stop!"

It was loud and clear this time, accompanied by her pushing at his shoulders with as much strength as she could muster with his hand buried in her pussy. Jerald immediately paused. He looked into her eyes, saw them slowly opening, trying to focus on him.

"I can't do this here. Not now," she said more steadily.

Jerald thought with a start about where they were, whether they were supposed to be here together or not and how out of control this desire for her had really become. He'd never wanted to fuck in an elevator before. Had never followed a female into a bathroom and damn sure had never threatened one over a text message.

What the hell was going on with him?

He pulled out of her, taking a quick step back simultaneously. Another step back and he felt like there was a safe distance between them.

"I'm sorry," he said, dragging a hand down his face.

The hand that had just been touching her. The scent of her arousal on his fingers had him gulping, his pulse still beating rapidly in his ears and his dick still throbbing. He dropped both hands to his side.

She fixed her clothes, then brushed at her hair.

"Don't apologize," she told him. "I wanted it. I mean, I don't know why but I did. But I can't do this right now. I have to stay focused. I have to get this job done without any interruptions."

"Is that what this is, Hailey? An interruption?" he asked her, a small part of him amazed that she'd been able to categorize what was tearing through him so simply, while he was still struggling to figure it out.

She looked up at him then. "Yes," she said quietly. "It is. You don't understand because you don't know me, Jerald. You don't know anything about me accept the fact that you like having sex with me."

She paused, took a breath and then continued. "There's more to me than sex. And if I weren't in the situation I was in now, I might be willing to let you find out. Even though I don't even know if that's your intention at all."

"I—" he began.

Hailey held up a hand to stop him. "No. Please don't give me some practiced explanation, or even a lie that you think I need to hear. Because I don't."

"Is he doing something to you, Hailey? Is he threatening you to make you stay? Blackmailing you maybe?" Jerald asked because he still wasn't completely sold on her simply being Mendoza's translator.

She frowned at him then, shaking her head. "I'm not sleeping with him for money. I'm not some paid piece of ass, if that's what you're thinking?"

He hated how she'd said it, hated that he'd actually thought that very thing.

"I'm just trying to understand. If it's simply that you need money for school, why don't you take out a student loan? Do you have any idea what type of man he really is?"

"No," she said adamantly. "And I don't really care. All I know is that I need this job. I need the money he's giving me because a student loan is not enough. It's not going to pay my grandmother's..." she paused then, clenching her lips together and taking what he thought were meant to be steadying breaths.

"Like I told you before," she continued. "I didn't do anything with you that I didn't want to. I decided, Jerald. Not you. Just like I'm deciding to take care of what's important to me first, before even considering anything else. It's my business and I know what I'm doing."

She turned her back to him then, moving over to look at the control panel.

"You know you pushed the alarm button. The fire department and hotel security's probably already on their way."

Jerald stood to the back of the elevator trying to digest all that she'd said to him when there was a jolt and the elevator began to move again. It was taking them down to the lobby he saw as the lighted numbers went lower and lower. He adjusted his clothes and waited for the doors to open, expecting, just like she said, to see the fire department and hotel security.

They were both mistaken.

When the doors to the elevator opened Ronnel Mendoza was standing there. Two very bulky men, arms folded over their chest behind him. Jerald kept his eyes on Mendoza.

Hailey was about to step out of the elevator first, when Jerald moved to stand beside her. They stepped out together when Ronnel immediately reached for her hand.

"Are you unharmed?" he asked her.

Before she could answer Jerald said. "She's safe, Mendoza. But your business is not. You have a week to make up your mind. Seven days before the Feds release a report of the findings from their investigation. Do you know what they're going to say, Mendoza? Do you know how that report is going to affect your already floundering company?" Jerald reached up to straighten his tie after that last question.

"I do," he finished when he saw Mendoza staring at him angrily. "I know exactly how it's going to affect you and the stocks of your company."

He smiled then, walking slowly towards the front door. Leaving Hailey with him and hopefully leaving Mendoza with something else to think about other than the fact that he and Hailey had been alone in that stalled elevator together.

Later that night as Jerald lay in his bed, sleep cleverly evading him, he decided to text Hailey to see if she was alright. He'd been waiting a half hour and she hadn't responded. Every part of him wanted to get up out of that bed, slip on his clothes and drive over to the Mendoza estate, but he knew that would be a mistake.

There was still a deal in play with Mendoza. Busting in his house and dragging Hailey out of there would most assuredly kill that deal in the water. Sure, Mendoza thought he wasn't going to do business with Carrington Enterprises, but he would. D&D Investigations had emailed Jerald a copy of the report that was going to be released next

Friday. He knew that once it hit the air and once Mendoza was arrested, his company would be up for grabs. He had to get Mendoza to make the deal with him before that happened.

Now, however, Hailey was also a factor.

She was in that house, working for him.

What would happen to her after Jerald closed the deal and Mendoza ended up in jail? How would she get the money she needed then? And what the hell did she need that money for?

Getting out of bed Jerald left his bedroom heading to his home office. He booted up his laptop and when it was ready typed in Hailey's name. He wanted to know everything there was to know about her. Everything she'd done in her life and most importantly everything she needed.

Why? He wondered even as he continued to read through the information from the first search he'd performed.

What did he plan to do with this information once he found it? And why the hell did it matter? She was just another woman. Right?

Wrong.

She was the one he'd slept with not once but twice, and the one he desperately wanted in his bed again.

CHAPTER 5

Jerald slammed his hands on the steering wheel. He was doing the right thing. At least he'd thought so an hour ago when he'd awakened from the most fitful night of sleep he'd experienced in too long to recall. He'd dressed for work in a navy blue suit and light blue shirt and just when he was about to put his tie on he thought of her again.

At the party on Friday Hailey had mentioned her grandmother, Katherine Glory Jefferson. She had not said anything about her grandfather, Arthur Marvin Jefferson. He died six years ago, around the time Hailey would have been graduating from high school. As far as his limited online searches could take him Jerald could not find any siblings and there were only old obituary listings from a funeral home in Maitlin, Virginia. Jean and Paul Jefferson were killed in a car accident. Hailey would have been seven years old at the time.

All weekend he'd thought about her, that seven year old girl that had lost her parents and was sent to live with her grandparents.

He pulled his cell phone from his pocket dialing a number without even thinking.

"Good Morning," he said the moment Noble finished his greeting. "I'm going to be in late. Have Mandi print the Makisig stock reports and I want the projections for Mendoza's accessories line on my desk when I get there."

"Jackson's back. He's in the office and already requested you meet with him regarding this deal. What do you want me to tell him?"

"Tell him I'll see him when I get there," Jerald replied.

"And when will that be?"

"About an hour or two."

"Is there something wrong? Something I can help with?" Noble continued.

Jerald had just started the engine and wanted to get moving as soon as possible. He did not want to go into the details of his personal life with his assistant. "No. Just do what I asked. I'll see you in a couple of hours."

He disconnected the call before Noble could ask another question. Jerald slipped his phone back into his pant pocket and pulled out of the parking spot in the garage. He had a lengthy drive ahead of him and he wanted to get there early.

As he drove, Jerald considered calling someone else. But then he'd thought better of it. Maybe this situation wasn't that serious to call in what Jackson had referred to just a few months ago as the top guns in the investigative field. Besides, this was a personal matter and Jerald always kept his personal life away from business.

Until now, he thought almost twenty minutes later when he'd finally made it out of the city. Mendoza was a big deal to Carrington Enterprises. At the same time—and for reasons he still wasn't ready to own up to—Hailey was a big deal to him.

For weeks, Jerald had watched only the recording he'd had of their night together on the beach. Totally disregarding the other twenty or so videos that he'd acquired over the last months during his appointments at The Corporation. He'd simply lost interest in watching anyone else.

A key factor to that decision could have been that during those other exploits he had never been as hard and undeniably aroused as he had been with Hailey. The second recording further proved that point as he'd grown obsessed with watching that one, loving the way she looked atop him, her heavy breasts jerking as she pumped.

That year after the accident, not only was Jerald going through rehabilitation to learn how to walk again, but he was also wondering if he'd ever receive an erection again. Not knowing had haunted him day and night as, at nineteen years old he was still filled with raging hormones. The urgings hadn't ceased which made the fact that there was no release in sight all the more painful. And as time had passed and he continued to lose hope, he'd taken to watching porn videos.

In the years after the accident, when he had finally been able to achieve an erection, with the aid of medication most times, he'd had sex with a female. But it wasn't like he'd experienced before and Jerald feared it never would be again. That's when he'd decided to deal only with professional women. Their autonomy and lack of expectations were just what he needed. It wasn't until he joined The Corporation, however, did the idea of videotaping those escapades come to mind. Each time he watched one of the videos, he figured, it confirmed that he had healed—to the best of his ability. He could get a hard-on without those little blue pills and he could achieve an orgasm as well as bring the same pleasure to a female.

But none of that—not the pills, the videos, the professional women he walked out the door without looking back, none of it—could compare to what he'd felt when he was with Hailey.

That's why he was driving well above the speed limit heading to the Mendoza estate at a little before eight on a Monday morning. It was also why he'd spent a good portion of the night learning more about her situation. Jerald wanted to help her. He wanted to get her away from Mendoza before anything could happen to her.

Once again, Jerald pulled to the side of the road just before the wrought iron gates leading up the hill to

Mendoza's house. He had no idea if or when Hailey would be coming out but suspected she wasn't the type to want to stay closed up in a house all day long. Something vibrant in her eyes and her easy smile made him think she was more the outgoing and adventurous type—two things he'd never prided himself on being. Maybe that was something else he liked about her.

What he definitely did not like was the way he'd begun to feel like an obsessed stalker where she was concerned. Whether he was sending her demanding text messages or pulling her into elevators, or even now, sitting on the side of the road waiting for her. Jerald knew things were getting out of hand. It was all so out of character for him that he felt like berating himself. Not only was Jerald Carrington not a man that begged, he had certainly never chased a woman in his life. The fact that this woman, out of all the people he'd ever known, had brought out this behavior in him was telling. It was obvious and then it was a mystery to him, as if he knew the answer, had known it all along but refused to accept it. In other words, he was screwed.

"Ten minutes and I'm out the door," Hailey yelled up the steps to Rhia who was still getting dressed.

"We're going to the beauty salon so I don't get why she's doing all that primping," Malaya who was sitting on the last step, playing a video game on her tablet said without looking up.

Hailey only half listened to the little girl as she held the keys in one hand while checking her cell phone for messages with the other. She was waiting on a call from her grandmother's doctor. Instead she found a text message from Ronnel telling her to have the girls back by noon. Skipping over the message she frowned as she recalled the complete shift in his mood in the last week.

It had started the day after she'd come from Jerald's house. That had been the first time that Ronnel had made any mention of her literally being at his beck and call. She grimaced as she remembered Jerald saying as much the other night in the elevator. But Ronnel had not wanted her to go anywhere or do anything other than be at the meetings with him and attend to his daughters. Giving her the instructions about the keys to the SUV had been a sure sign of that. She'd taken that and the way he'd begun popping up as if he were checking on her with the girls, as part of the job. She didn't have to like it. Hell, most people didn't like some aspect of their jobs, but it still paid the bills. So she'd sucked it up figuring she only had a couple more months to go and then she'd look back and it would all be worth it.

Friday night, after the party at the Ritz Carlton, however, Ronnel had pushed another button that annoyed the hell out of her.

"Do not be with him," he'd said the moment they were in the house.

The entire limo ride had been in silence, with her sitting on one side of the backseat starring out the window and him on the other. Her mind had been circling around everything she'd said to Jerald and why the hell she couldn't seem to stay away from him. If truth be told, he was the one who had insisted she come with him. But in the end, she'd made the decision to go. He hadn't picked her up, carried or dragged her for that matter. Just as it had happened on the island and when he'd sent her that text message, Hailey had gone of her own free will.

What did that mean?

Did she really want to be this guy's mistress? Was sex with him worth sinking low enough to be considered someone's side chick? Because, without a doubt Hailey knew that's what she would be. For one, it wasn't as if Jerald were begging her to go out on a date. No, he was just persistent as hell—and all too convincing—when it came to getting her so sexually excited that she couldn't think of nothing else but jumping into bed with him. And two, she was clearly not in the same league with the Carringtons, or anyone else that had been at that party the other night. To be perfectly honest it was the first time Hailey had even been in a Ritz Carlton, let alone on its rooftop loft for a party of some fancy movie producer. She'd found that out later that night when Rhia had come into her room asking about the dresses and the hairstyles she'd seen at the party.

At any rate, Jerald Carrington was not the man for her.

But she'd be damned if she'd let Ronnel Mendoza, her employer, tell her this.

"You do not belong with him. I make payments to you," he told her in his very best broken English.

Perhaps because she'd been standing in the foyer staring at him as if he had lost some part of his damn mind.

"I was not with him," she'd replied, trying to hold on to every piece of respect and patience she could.

As a child Hailey had always had a quick temper. Pops said that came from her grandmother, but she'd never seen Gram so much as raise her voice at Pops. During her elementary and middle school years she'd even had problems with back-talking to her teachers and other students. It seemed that whenever she was provoked she'd reply in turn. Until the day one of her teachers called Gram up to the school. Her grandmother—the one who supposedly had the same bad temper—had not yelled or even looked at Hailey in a cross way. What she did was take her home and wash her mouth out with the bar of Ivory soap that sat in a dish beside the kitchen sink. As Hailey cried, soap bubbles foaming at her mouth, Gram had simply said, "You'd better learn to hold your tongue before something far worse than a good cleansing happens to it."

Hailey hadn't known what that meant at the time, but she did know she didn't want that awful taste in her mouth ever again. From that point on she'd learned to do just as Gram had said and hold her tongue until it was absolutely necessary to do otherwise.

Tonight, that restraint would come in handy.

"He is a thief!" Ronnel continued pulling the scarf roughly from his neck and clenching the material in his hands when they'd entered the house. "He think he can take everything I have. My company. *Mi mujer*. No. I will not allow him!"

He'd called her *his woman* and Hailey had immediately blanched. She was not his woman. Did he think that just because he was paying her? Why not? Hadn't Jerald thought the same thing?

"I am here to translate for you and your daughters," she'd spoken in as calm a voice as she could muster in an attempt to set the record straight. "That is all."

"Then you do as I say," he'd immediately shot back.

"I will do my job," had been her response before turning away and walking up the steps.

She hadn't run, but walked just in case he thought he had something else to say. Hailey had no idea how she was going to react if he had. Was she going to lose her temper and, in turn, this job. Oh goodness, she hoped the hell not.

And she hadn't. Ronnel sent her an apology text early the next morning and had kept his distance throughout the entire weekend, but he'd made certain he knew exactly where she was with the girls and had even begun giving them timeframes to come back. It was an act of control. Hailey knew this, just as she knew she had no other choice but to go along with. As long as he didn't touch her and didn't declare her his *mujer* again, these weeks would go by without a hitch. She would get her money and get the hell away from him and from Jerald Carrington. As both men were driving her just a little bit crazy.

LaChic Salon was an upscale beauty palace, as Rhia had described it. She'd talked for days about all the girls she knew that went there to have their hair colored. It had been a place she just "had" to go to, as she'd told her father during the twenty minute performance earlier in the week.

Ronnel was very indulgent when it came to his daughters. Hailey suspected that was because he was a single parent and at that moment wondered once again what had happened to his wife. The girls never spoke of their mother and Hailey hadn't wanted to ask.

So on Ronnel's orders Hailey had made an appointment for the girls and she was now accompanying them, not sure what to expect when she walked through the glass doors. There was glass everywhere, was her immediate thought. All of the front windows and mirrors throughout what she realized was only the first floor of the salon. There was a black and white theme going with black leather salon chairs at stations with black lacquer stands. In the center of the room was a round black and white zebra striped couch and pop music blared from speakers she couldn't see.

"I've already checked us in," a very excited Rhia said and Hailey realized she hadn't even seen the girl walk away from her.

She really needed to pay more attention. These last couple of days her mind had been on so many other things that she'd been missing stuff like the fact that Rhia had apparently snuck out late last night. Malaya had, of course, told on her sister this morning while Hailey sat in the kitchen having a cup of coffee. At that time she'd been thinking of how much it would cost to enroll for her classes and at the same time how good it would feel knowing that they were the *last* classes before she graduated.

"Ok, well we can just sit over here and wait to be called," she told them and was just about to take a step towards that crazy looking couch when she heard someone call her name.

The three of them turned at the same time but only Hailey recognized the man standing in the doorway. It was almost surreal the way the glare of the sun served as a backdrop to what could have easily been a million dollar photo. Perhaps it would be titled "The Sexy Side of Business".

Jerald stood dressed in a suit, his right hand in his pant pocket, holding that half of his jacket back so that the slim fit of the shirt he wore and the intricate paisley design on his tie was also visible. He looked like a movie star about to deliver his most epic line in a flick.

"What are you doing here?" she asked walking up to him immediately. "I'm working and I told you last night—"

He lifted two fingers, putting them very close to her lips but not touching her. She clapped her mouth closed anyway.

"I just need to talk to you for a few minutes. I think I know how to help you out of this situation," he told her.

"What situation?" Rhia asked from beside her.

"He smells good," Malaya added with a smile as she came to stand at Hailey's other side.

"Nothing," Hailey replied quickly, looking at both girls. "You two go on over and have a seat. I'll just be a minute."

Rhia looked at her with a knowing grin. "He asked for a *few* minutes, to be exact." She leaned in closer to whisper, "He's hot so you should give him whatever he wants!"

Hailey sighed inwardly as the young girl's words echoed true to some extent in her mind. Hadn't she been giving Jerald sex when he wanted it because he was, as Rhia had said, "hot" and her body just could not resist his?

"Go. Now," she reiterated then waited impatiently while they both walked away.

Malaya had turned back, covering her mouth and unsuccessfully disguising the giggles that erupted as she looked from Jerald to Hailey once more.

"Are you crazy?" she asked the moment she was alone with Jerald.

He took her by the arm then, walking so they were further away from the receptionist's desk where two ladies were staring at them with as much interest as Rhia and Malaya had just shown. For that reason alone she did not argue with him pulling her to the side. Still, the moment they were a safe hearing distance away from the desk—

thanks in part to the loud music blaring throughout the place—Hailey pulled her arm away.

"Are you stalking me now? How did you know I was here?" she asked, trying to keep her voice lowered.

"You told my mother you were going to finish college in the next year. And then you mentioned something about your grandmother as you were trying to defend working for Mendoza," he began, not really trying to lower his voice at all.

He wasn't a loud talker, so she supposed nobody else could hear him anyway. Still, the way he was standing so casually in front of her as if him walking in here and demanding to speak with her was actually normal on some level, irritated her.

Shaking her head she continued pressing him, not at all pleased by his arrival or what he had to say to her. "I asked you a question first. Are you stalking me? Is that what millionaires do here in L.A.? Stalk women they've had sex with but have been told to leave alone?"

Her heart was beating rampantly, but not with any shred of fear. If Jerald was a stalker, he was doing a piss-poor job of frightening her. Yet, that muscle that twitched on the left side of his jaw never failed to arouse her.

"I'm not a stalker. I'm simply trying to help you," was his steady reply. "I know that your grandfather passed away several years ago and I presume you've been trying to help your grandmother since that time. Is that why it's taken you so long to finish college?"

She must have been looking at him like he'd lost his mind, she was certainly thinking that at this very moment.

"Hailey, listen to me, Mendoza is not who you think he is. He's into some pretty bad things and I'm just trying to protect you from getting caught up in them."

"What?" Hailey couldn't get out anymore words. Her temples throbbed as she tried to figure out what the hell was going on.

Was Jerald really standing here warning her about the guy she'd begun to think of as some sort of savior?

"Look, I know you have business with him. So I guess that's why you figure you can look into my background the same way you did his. But I can assure you that I have no sway with him at all. I just go to the meetings to translate anything he cannot understand. I don't advise him on his business in any way," she told him.

"I don't care about that. I know how to work my deal with Mendoza," he said and for the first time began to look as irritated and confused as Hailey was feeling.

He lifted a hand to rub along his chin, smoothing down the neatly shaved goatee as he continued to watch her.

"I want to help you. If you need money I'll give it to you. Just quit this job with Mendoza and do it now," he insisted.

"You can't tell me to quit my job," she replied vehemently. "That's not your place, nor is it any of your concern."

"He's going to be arrested, Hailey," Jerald said quickly. Then he cursed and sighed heavily. "The Feds found some pretty damning information on him and they're going to be closing in on him just as soon as all the warrants are in place. My guess is that'll be in the next two or three days. So as much as I do enjoy having sex with you, what I'm offering has nothing to do with that. I want to keep you safe."

Two seconds after he'd said those words Hailey saw a car come screeching to a halt just outside of the salon. The window rolled down and the next thing she saw was the glass to the front window of the salon shattering. Jerald's arms went around her instantly as he was propelled forward. She lost her footing and they both fell to the floor, glass raining down over them.

His back screamed in agony, chest lifting and falling as
he struggled to take a good breath. She was in his arms,
Jerald knew that for a fact because the warmth of her body
melded with his own. But she was still as a statue so he had
no idea if grabbing her and falling on top of her had
protected her the way he'd intended to.

Jerald looked down only to be startled to see Hailey was
looking up at him. Her eyes were wide with shock, her hair
a mass of confusion surrounding her face. And there was
blood. On her forehead and her cheek and Jerald frowned.

"Are you alright? Can you move?" he asked her.

She blinked and nodded. "I think so. I mean, if you
move I can probably get up too."

Right.

He was just starting to move when the two girls who had
flocked to her side when he'd come in appeared once more.

"What happened? Get off of her," the younger one
yelled. "Get off her so she can breathe!"

The little girl was yelling and so was someone else close
by. One of those receptionists with the multiple piercings
he suspected.

"Call an ambulance!" he heard someone else cry as he
moved off of Hailey.

Bracing his hands on the floor he stayed on his knees for
a couple moments longer than he wanted. Pain radiated
down his back and he wasn't positive he'd be able to stand
without falling to the ground once more, this time without
the excuse of protecting Hailey.

He looked up just in time to see the two girls helping
Hailey from the floor, bits of glass cracking beneath their
feet as they moved. What the hell had just happened?

"Jerald, you're hurt," Hailey said coming to stand beside
him, her hands gripping his arms as she tried to help him
up.

"No. I'm fine," he said using every bit of strength he had
to stand and sending up a silent prayer that he wouldn't
topple over when he did.

"What happened?" one of the receptionists, the taller one he surmised as he finally stood up straight, had come over to them by now.

"Somebody threw that brick through the window," the younger girl said pointing to the brick lying on the floor right next to where he and Hailey had fallen.

"It smacked you right in the back," the older girl that had been with Hailey said.

She'd come to stand at his other side, touching a hand to his arm as if she wanted to help him, but was afraid of what he might say. Jerald managed a smile down at her before he looked over to Hailey.

"I'm fine, really. But you're bleeding," he replied lifting a hand to her forehead.

There were small specks of blood where the shards of flying glass most likely hit her. He frowned again as his efforts to wipe them away only ended up smearing the blood across the light tone of her skin.

"The ambulance is on the way and so are the police," the other receptionist said. "You two should sit down until they get here."

When Jerald moved so did the pain in his back and for a moment he thought...he remembered...and he feared. Gritting his teeth he continued moving until he sat on the zebra print sofa, Hailey sitting down right beside him. She had a hand on his shoulder and one on his thigh.

"That brick hit you in the back. Let me take off your jacket and see how bad it is," she said as she began to push at the lapel of his suit jacket.

"No," Jerald said adamantly, shaking his head to make sure she heard him just in case the pain had actually taken his voice. "It's good. Don't worry about it."

"It's not good. You're wincing every time you move," she told him.

Jerald managed a smile, or at least he thought it was an upward tilt of his lips. "Then I won't move anymore."

"It says something," the younger girl was yelling from where she still stood near the door. "Something's written on this brick."

"Don't touch it!" the older girl yelled at her, smacking her hand so that the brick fell to the floor again.

Hailey got up and went to the girls. "You two come back over here," she told them. "Go and sit with Mr. Carrington."

Jerald saw her look down to the brick and frown.

"What does it say?" he asked the second the two girls sat beside him.

Hailey didn't reply but gave him a weird look instead.

"It says CHEATER," the younger girl announced.

"Are you by chance cheating on someone, Mr. Carrington?" the older one asked.

The pain in his neck Jerald incurred from looking back and forth between the two girls only aggravated the pain still searing up and down his back.

"No. I am not cheating on anyone," he answered them, then looked over to Hailey with a raised brow.

She shook her head as if she had to tell him not to mention Mendoza and the warning he'd been trying to give her earlier. Jerald didn't need her to tell him that. He'd figured these two little girls were Mendoza's daughters and had no intention of saying anything that they might take back to their father.

The paramedics came through the door first, two police cars pulling up right behind the ambulance, officers from the LAPD immediately stepping out onto the street. Two officers stayed outside and immediately began pushing the growing crowd back away from the salon, while the other two came inside, following behind the paramedics.

"He's hurt," Hailey had told them and rushed back over to where he sat with the paramedics in tow. "The brick hit him in the back."

"It's not a problem," Jerald began when one of the paramedics had already put down their bag and knelt in front of him.

"Let's just have a look," he said and Jerald tensed.

"No," he replied immediately.

"Can you tell us what happened?" a police officer asked.

"We were just standing there talking and I saw a car pull up. The next thing I know the windows are breaking and we fell to the floor. That's all I know," Hailey volunteered.

"And what's your name?" the officer that had been scribbling on his notepad asked.

"I'm Hailey Jefferson."

"And this is Mr. Carrington. His back is hurting but he's trying to act like it's not. Boys are so silly. They never want anyone to know when they're hurt. But I can tell. Just like when Abnez Cortez fell off his bike back in day camp when I was a little girl," the younger Mendoza girl said with a shake of her head.

"We can go back to the truck and take a look, if you'd like Mr. Carrington?" the paramedic told him.

The other paramedic had gone over to Hailey and was now shinning a light in her eyes and asking her questions. She was answering him and the cop without flinching while Jerald sat on this couch acting like…well, as this little girl had just said, a silly boy.

Clearing his throat he stood. "Sure. Let's go," Jerald told the paramedic.

"There's something written on that brick so there may be some fingerprints," he told the officer that was talking to Hailey. I'm going to need your written report by the end of business today."

When the officer looked at him in question, Jerald simply reached into his inside jacket pocket and pulled out his business card. "Send it directly to me by email and tell Commissioner Francois I said hello."

He gave the officer his card and watched as he read his name, just seconds before he mentioned the police

commissioner who had, coincidentally, been at the
Renquist party on Friday night.

"He's going to the hospital, Hailey. We should go with
him," the little girl who was once again at his side said.

Jerald never wanted children, had never even thought
about them except from the distance of someone's pictures
or as part of an overheard office conversation. But here he
was, standing in the middle of a beauty shop that had just
been vandalized in what he thought might be a personal
attack on Hailey, with this little girl twining her fingers in
his.

"I don't think—" Hailey began.

"It's a good idea," he interrupted. "You can get checked
out too.

"I'm fine. I can just drive the girls home and get cleaned
up there," she continued.

"You should get checked out ma'am, just to make sure
everything is alright," one of the paramedics added.

"Why don't we all head down to the hospital and I can
get statements from all of you," an officer finally stated
with irritation.

CHAPTER 6

Where are you?
What's going on?
On the television it says there's been some sort of incident? What is happening?
One text message after another and another. Hailey's head throbbed and her hands were still shaking on the steering wheel as she followed the ambulance to the hospital. Ronnel had been texting her since they'd climbed into the SUV. And she hadn't answered him. When the phone rang she'd ignored that too. He would yell and order her to get to the house as soon as possible and Hailey just did not feel like hearing it at the moment. She was fine and so were the girls. Jerald wasn't.

Hailey was certain of that fact and it was making her extremely irritable.

"Call your father and let him know you're alright," she told Rhia who was sitting across from her.

Malaya was in the backseat still pouting because she'd wanted to ride in the ambulance with Jerald. Since she wasn't the injured party and was not over twenty-one, that hadn't been allowed, but Jerald had promised to drive her home. That had seemed to make her happy until she'd climbed into the truck with Hailey and Rhia.

Rhia didn't respond to Hailey's request.

"Did you hear what I said?" Hailey asked, looking at her quickly, then back to the road.

Traffic was horrible, even if she was tailing the ambulance.

"She doesn't hear anything you're saying because she's texting that guy she snuck out of the house to see last night," Malaya offered.

Rhia grumbled something and turned back momentarily to give Malaya a snarl. With a huff she settled back in her seat and her fingers moved quickly over her phone once more.

"If you're texting anyway, it'll only take you a second to let him know we're fine," she told Rhia.

"I'll do it in a minute," the girl snapped. "He wants to know that I'm alright too, so I'm telling him what happened."

"He?" Hailey asked. "The guy you snuck out to see last night? The guy that called the house and you fell in love with his voice?"

"You make it sound like I'm making him up," Rhia replied.

Hailey sighed, turning the corner, thankful that the hospital was now at least in sight.

"I don't think you're making him up," Hailey told her. "But I do think that maybe you should let your father meet this guy. How old is he anyway? And why are you being so secretive about him? You haven't even told me his name."

Not that Hailey had been overly interested in Rhia's love life. She was having a hell of a time trying to keep her own in line. Hell, she'd never even thought she'd have a love life, let alone have the need to keep it in order. Things were getting so out of hand. And now this. Who the hell threw that brick and why did it say CHEATER? Was Jerald involved with someone?

That would be just great, she thought with a heavy sigh. She'd slept with someone else's man and now that woman was getting her revenge. But if that were the case why would she have thrown the brick at Jerald and not her?

"I'm sending him the text," Rhia said finally. "Satisfied?"

She'd thrust the phone across the console so Hailey could see the text she'd just sent to her father.

"Thank you," Hailey said too tired and too confused to argue as she pulled into the spot right next to the ambulance in the hospital parking lot.

Twenty minutes later she'd just finished listening to the discharge instructions from the nurse—come back to the ER if she feels dizzy or nauseous and all that good stuff—Hailey was preparing to leave this room and gather up the girls. It was well after noon now and she was certain Ronnel was about to lose his mind because they weren't there.

The minute she'd stepped out into the hallway he was there. Tall and broad shouldered, just like Jerald. A little lighter complexioned, more hair—dark and curly on top, low-cut on the sides—mustache, beard and furrowed brows. Yes, that's what caught her attention, he was angry and there was no doubt about that.

"Hailey Jefferson?" he asked taking a step towards her.

She cleared her throat and replied, "Yes", even though she really wanted to employ that childhood warning to never speak to strangers.

"I'm Jackson Carrington," he said coming to a stop in front of her, his hand extended.

She looked down at it for a moment, before coming to her senses and shaking his hand. "Is Jerald alright?"

"He's getting a prescription for the pain but the doctor said he'll be fine in a day or two."

"That's good," she said with a sigh. "Well, I have to go now."

He nodded but did not step out of her way. "You have to take Rhia and Malaya Mendoza home. Is that correct?"

"Yes," she replied not liking the tone of his voice or the way he continued to glower down at her. "If you'll excuse me."

Jackson shook his head. "Not just yet. Ronnel Mendoza is a pretty sleazy character and if my company did not stand to benefit tremendously from taking over his, I wouldn't have anything to do with that scum."

"That's none of my business," she replied and attempted to move around him.

She'd heard everything Jerald had to say about Ronnel and was still determined not to get involved in this aspect of her employer's life. This was just a job, she reminded herself.

This time Jackson actually clamped his hands around her arms to hold her in place. It wasn't hard and, just as with Jerald, she did not feel any sense of fear from this man. However, she did want him to get away from her and leave her alone.

"Look, Mr. Carrington. I've told your brother this and now I guess I have to tell you too. I only work for Mr. Mendoza. It's a summer job and when it's done I'll be returning home to Virginia. I do not need to know about your business dealings with him or his personal life as I'm just his translator."

"You're a young female living under his roof which places you in grave danger," he told her seriously. "Do you know what happened to Sherizia Mendoza? That was the mother of his children and she looked a lot like the oldest daughter, Rhia, when she was twenty years old. That's how old she was when she was last seen, just a year after giving birth to Malaya. Nobody has seen or heard from her again."

Hailey hadn't known Sherizia Mendoza and she hadn't thought for one moment about why she wasn't there with her family. Okay, well, yes, she had, but still, it didn't matter. It was none of her business.

"Mr. Carrington—" she began but he quickly cut her off.

"He likes his women young and trainable. Pretty and compliant," he said looking her up and down until Hailey felt so self-conscious that she yanked her arms free and took a few defensive steps back from him.

"I'm not his woman," she told him, trying to sound confident. Instead her voice had seemed small and uncertain and she frowned.

"You're something," Jackson continued coming closer to her once more. "And whatever you are it's brought violence to my brother. Now, I'm going to tell you this one time and one time only. If you don't plan to walk away from Mendoza, then stay the hell away from Jerald. Things are going to get pretty dicey with Mendoza and his company in the upcoming days so you need to decide which side you're going to end up on because I won't let you drag my brother into this and I won't let you get him killed because of some childish game you wish to play."

Hailey felt aptly scolded. No, dammit, she felt totally pissed off. Was this guy really in her face blaming her for what just happened to Jerald, to both of them for that matter? Did he really think she was sleeping with Mendoza and messing with Jerald at the same time? What kind of crazy and distrustful men were these Carringtons anyway?

"First of all," she said stepping forward so that she was closer to him this time.

He wore a black suit with a crisp yellow tie and looked every bit as formidable as she figured he probably was. Still, Hailey didn't care. He didn't know her and so had no reason to speak to her the way he was.

"I'm not the one that cannot stay away from your brother. He's the one following me around town and looking into my background. I told him I couldn't see him because I was working for Mendoza. Working—by the way, not sleeping with him the way you and your brother's sordid little minds seem to work. You'd think all a woman was good for was sex according to you two!"

"Ms. Jefferson," he started.

"No! Don't Ms. Jefferson me," she said, anger rolling through her like a steam train. "First your brother follows me around giving me all these orders telling me what to do and who not to do it with and now you. I don't work for either of you, nor do I give a damn about your business dealings. So, Mr. Carrington, if you would kindly get out of my way and stay away from me, I'll do the same with you and your brother. Thank you very much."

She pushed past him this time, not caring if she knocked him down. He was strong and built like an NFL player and probably had bodyguards, even though she hadn't seen any, just like Ronnel did. Still, Hailey didn't care, she was on her way down the hall when two more men stopped her. She felt like screaming but instead fisted her hands at her sides.

"Come over here so I can talk to you for a moment," Jerald said.

He was wearing a different shirt, a dark t-shirt that even though it did not go with the dress pants and shiny tie-ups he was wearing, still managed to make him look dangerously sexy. There was another guy standing just behind him, a slim man with glasses who held a plastic hospital bag which Hailey figured held Jerald's jacket, dress shirt and tie.

"Please, Jerald. I'm tired of this. First you, then your brother, and now you again. I just really need to get the girls home," she pleaded.

"I know," he said with a knowing nod. "I just have one thing to say to you and then you can go. In fact, I'll drive Malaya home just like I promised."

"You really shouldn't drive, Mr. Carrington," the man behind him said. "The doctor gave you pain medication remember?"

Jerald frowned but did not turn back to look at or scold the man which Hailey thought he probably wanted to do. "Just one minute?" he asked, reaching a hand out to gently touch her arm.

Hailey sighed. "One minute, Jerald and that's it."

He was nodding as they moved a little further down the hall to a small alcove that housed two vending machines.

"Look, before you say anything, just let me apologize," he said when they were alone and facing each other. "I shouldn't have looked into your background and I shouldn't have followed you today. I just—I, hell, Hailey I don't know why I did it," he said finally with a sigh. "All I know is that I want to keep you safe. I didn't believe you at first when you said you were only working as Mendoza's translator, but I know that's true now. Just like I know you desperately need money. And I meant what I said about wanting to help you."

Hailey shook her head. His words had been successful at rubbing like a salve against the red-hot anger his brother had provoked, and that pissed her off. No, it confused her even more. She didn't know what to think or to say about all that had happened, all that she'd learned today. It was beginning to be too much.

"I understand," she started but then shook her head again. "No, I don't. I've never been in this situation before, Jerald. And it's not why I came to L.A. I didn't plan for any of this and now I feel like it's spiraling out of control."

"I know, sweetheart, I know and I apologize for making things worst," he told her, this time taking her by the shoulders and pulling her close for a hug.

Hailey didn't want to hug him, but then she did. She'd been so worried on the ride to the hospital about his injuries. The worry was intense and was what really had prevented her from calling or texting Ronnel. On some level she'd felt like that would have been a betrayal to Jerald. It was silly, she knew, but she was chalking the crazy thoughts up to remnants of the traumatic events she'd just endured.

When she stopped thinking and wrapped her arms around him he winched and she immediately jerked back.

"I'm so sorry, are you okay?"

He nodded. "It's going to be fine as soon as those pain killers kick in."

Hailey sighed and blinked as his intense green gaze held hers captive. She didn't want to move, not one muscle. She wanted to stay right here enveloped in the warmth of his embrace, looking up into eyes that seemed only to see her.

"What are we doing?" she whispered.

"I don't know," he admitted with a heavy sigh. "I have no idea."

After a few more seconds of staring and not knowing she started to pull away. "I should go."

"Yes," he replied but still did not release her. "Have dinner with me."

His words were quick and out of the blue and she wasn't sure she'd actually heard them until he repeated himself.

"Just dinner and we'll talk. I feel like we've never really had a chance to do that before," he said.

And he was right. They'd had sex, deliciously hot and soul-shattering sex and they'd argued. But they'd never talked.

She opened her mouth to reply, not at all certain what she was going to say but he cut her off anyway.

"Don't answer right now. Let's get you and the girls home and we'll both get some rest. We can talk about the when and where of our dinner date later."

"That sounds like a good idea," Hailey said because since she had no idea what her answer was going to be, stalling for more time to figure it out was the perfect plan.

They did not arrive at the Mendoza estate until well after two in the afternoon. Traffic out of the city was slow going and the girls were in a peculiar mood. Rhia had been quiet all the way back to the house, but when they'd pulled to the side of the road just before the front gates so that Malaya could get out of Jerald's car and into the SUV, her mood grew even darker.

"You're going to get in trouble," Rhia told Malaya as she settled into the backseat.

Jerald had stood near his car, offering a stiff wave that mimicked the one Hailey had given him through the side mirror. She'd pulled off immediately after that and was just turning through the gates when her attention zoomed in on the girls.

"He doesn't like us speaking to strangers. That's why he always hires someone to be with us at all times," Rhia was saying.

"You're speaking to a stranger," Malaya shot back. "Calling and texting that guy and sneaking out to meet him. If you tell on me I'll tell on you."

"Nobody's going to tell on anyone," Hailey told them quickly.

She was turning into the courtyard, bringing the SUV to a stop. Putting the vehicle in park she turned sideways in her seat so that she could see both of them.

"A lot has happened today," she began then looked specifically at Rhia. "And last night."

"It was no big deal. I wanted to see him and he said he was close by. I was only gone for an hour," Rhia continued.

"An hour and a half. I heard when you came back," Malaya added.

"Nosey little brat!" Rhia yelled and attempted to reach into the backseat to get at her younger sister.

Hailey put an arm up in front of Rhia to stop her. "If this guy really likes you, he needs to come to the door and meet your father," she told her. And since Hailey suspected this guy was either too old for Rhia or not nearly as interested in a real relationship as much as she was—or possibly both—she kept eye contact with the teenager as she spoke.

"If he cannot or will not do that, then he's not worth your time. Respect is a very important part of a relationship, Rhia. A guy that asks you to sneak around and lie to your parents doesn't respect you."

She sounded like her Gram, Hailey thought with a pang of guilt and homesickness combined. Hadn't she been sneaking around with Jerald?

"He's too old for her," Malaya chimed in. "He has a real job and everything."

"Shut! Up!" Rhia yelled.

"Both of you be quiet," Hailey said, the headache that had been making a slow and steady appearance since they'd left the hospital was throbbing in full force now. "We're going to go into that house and let your father see that you are both alright. When he asks what happened we'll tell him the truth—someone threw a brick into the salon window. We've all been checked out at the hospital and we're all just fine."

"Right," Rhia said with a nod, her eyes boring into Hailey's. "And we won't tell him about Jerald Carrington from Carrington Enterprises showing up to speak with you. Or the fact that he touched you and stood very close to you as if he were used to doing that all the time."

"Or that someone wrote "CHEATER" on that brick that came crashing through the window," Malaya added.

Why these two little witches, Hailey thought as her headache intensified.

"Correct," she said, not caring how it sounded or made her look in their eyes. "We will not tell him that part."

Rhia nodded. "Because any guy that makes you lie for him doesn't respect you."

She hopped out of the SUV before Hailey could say another word and Hailey sighed.

"Don't worry," Malaya told her as she undid her seatbelt and reached for the door handle. "We're used to keeping secrets."

Hailey thought about those words as she followed the girls into the house, closing the door behind them. Loud voices coming from the living room stopped each of them as they wondered what was going on.

"It figures," Rhia finally said after it seemed like they'd been standing there forever. "We don't have to worry about lying to him. He doesn't give a damn what happened to us, that's why he didn't bother to come and see about us himself. It's always business first with him. Always has been."

She moved first, heading up the steps without looking back. Hailey still stood where she was listening to the voices speaking in Filipino, arguing about money and the *paninda*. She recognized Ronnel's voice loud and clear telling someone to sell all the *paninda*, the merchandise, immediately. That they needed all the money now. It hadn't dawned on her that she was eavesdropping or the reason why she'd felt so inclined to listen in on this business conversation until Malaya touched her arm.

"I won't tell about Mr. Carrington, Hailey," she whispered. "Because if I do, *tatay* will be angry." The little girl looked down at her feet, as she said in an even quieter tone. *"Makikita niya saktan ka kung gumawa siya ng galit mo."*

Malaya moved away from her then, running up the stairs her sister had just taken before Hailey could ask her what she'd meant. Everything Jerald had said to her about Ronnel replayed instantly through her mind as she stared towards the living room, toward the loud voices.

He'd warned her that Ronnel was not the man she thought he was, that he was dangerous and was going to be arrested for his crimes. Even his brother Jackson—even though he hadn't appeared half as concerned for her as he was his brother—had alluded to how dangerous Ronnel was. And she hadn't believed either of them, not at first. But now...

"Magandang hapon," a male voice said, effectively snapping Hailey out of her thoughts.

She looked up at him. He was standing close to her and she hadn't even heard his approach.

"Good afternoon," she repeated in English, taking a defensive step backward.

"You are the translator," he replied in stilted English.

Hailey nodded. "Yes. I am."

"She is just going to her room," Ronnel announced then, coming up behind the other man.

There was an ugly scar on this man's arm, a long gash that appeared to be healing on its own with jagged puffs of skin still read and bruised.

"Now, Hailey," Ronnel said, this time with more force.

She could tell him that she'd actually intended to go to the kitchen first to get something to drink so she could take some aspirin, but that didn't seem important at the moment. What seemed to make the most sense was that she actually listen to Ronnel and get the hell out of this room. She didn't like the way that guy was looking at her, the eerie smile spreading across his face made her feel sick and she wondered briefly if he'd done more than smile at another woman that way and she'd replied by stabbing him in the arm. If she had a weapon, Hailey was certain that's what she would do if he made another step towards her.

Instead she looked to Ronnel, saw his eyes, darker now than she'd ever seen them before, and the thin line of his lips as he continued to glare at her.

Makikita niya saktan ka kung gumawa siya ng galit mo.
He'll hurt you if you make him angry.

That's what Malaya had said to her before going upstairs. Hailey stared at Ronnel another second. He definitely looked angry. With a quick nod she made her way up the steps. Not running as she really wanted to, but taking each step with a quick stride until she was safely behind the door of her bedroom. She locked the door quickly then went to the bed, dropping down on it and wondering what the hell she'd gotten herself into.

CHAPTER 7

"Who is she?" Jackson asked as he sat on the couch in Jerald's living room. "Who is this Hailey Jefferson and why are you so attached to her?"

Jerald wished he could answer those questions.

He hadn't been at all surprised when he'd stepped out of the shower and heard the knock at the door, to see Jackson standing on the other side. His brother had been beyond pissed off when he'd arrived at the hospital this afternoon. Although he hadn't thought Jackson would be so upset that he'd bring Noble with him. As a rule the Carrington brothers were discreet, especially when it came to each other. But Jerald figured if there had to be someone else there, it was better that it was Noble and not his parents, especially since Noble had thought enough to bring him a change of clothes.

"She was at the meeting I had with Mendoza. She's his translator," Jerald replied, walking through his living room and heading back up the steps to his bedroom to get dressed.

Jackson would either fix himself a drink and wait, or…Jerald heard his brother following him up the steps.

"So she works for him?" Jackson continued. "How long? And what else does she do for him? I went through that file three times before I left and again last night. There's no mention of her in Mendoza's business or personal file."

Jerald went straight to his bureau, pulling open a drawer and taking out an undershirt first, then a pair of boxers. He turned to Jackson then and replied, "I know. She started working for him about six weeks ago. It's a summer job."

He moved into the bathroom after that, dropping the towel and putting his underwear on while hearing his brother swearing from the other room.

"She's not a danger to the deal," Jerald told him upon returning to the room. Then he cursed.

He'd left the towel on the bathroom floor. Something he never did. Running a hand down his face he took a deep breath and went back into the bathroom to retrieve the towel. Dropping it inside the hamper across from his bed he looked up to see his brother staring strangely at him.

"What? I said she's not a threat," Jerald reiterated.

He pushed past Jackson and went to his bed where he'd already laid out his clothes. Another suit, this time a coffee color with a pale blue shirt and royal tie. His shoes were at the end of the bed, right beneath where the suit lay neatly, brown Gucci lace ups.

"You know that for a fact?" Jackson inquired.

His brother stood with his arms folded over his chest, one hand lifted as he ran it over his bearded chin. He didn't believe Jerald. He knew something was going on. Jerald didn't bother to frown. Of the three Carrington brothers he was the most reserved, the quiet and solemn one. He could also be the most transparent one when something was wrong.

"Can you at least let me get dressed before we do this?" he asked, unable to hide the irritation in his tone.

"Before we do what, little brother? Before you finally open up and tell me what the hell has been going on with you these past few months?"

Jerald did not like when Jackson called him little brother. And he especially did not like the tone his brother was taking with him, that big-brother-to-the-rescue tone.

"I'll be downstairs in a few minutes," Jerald said not budging from where he stood and in that stance, with his own tone, making it quite clear that he wasn't going to talk anymore until he was dressed. And properly shielded, he thought.

Jackson walked towards the door. "You get ten minutes or I'm coming back and I'm not leaving until I get some answers."

Jerald walked across the room not bothering to look back at his brother. "Don't drink all my vodka," he warned. "It's too early in the day to get drunk."

Jackson never drank too much, at least not since he was in high school and had to be driven home by the bartender at the country club that recognized him. His brother hated losing control, even more so than Jerald did. But Jackson's favorite drink was vodka and cranberry. Jerald preferred his vodka straight and strong.

Fifteen minutes later, because he'd also stopped to check his emails, Jerald walked into his living room to see his brother sitting on his couch, the suit jacket he'd been wearing tossed over the backside of the chair.

"How long have you been sleeping with her?" Jackson asked him before Jerald could lay his suit jacket on the chair across from his brother's.

He went to the floor-to-ceiling windows, staring out at the bright sunny afternoon before replying, "Twice in six weeks." Many more times in his mind, but Jerald wisely kept that to himself.

"She's just trying to make some extra money so she can finish school," he continued, turning to face his brother then. "She has no idea what Mendoza's capable of."

"You're positive about that?" Jackson asked. "You're 100% sure that Mendoza isn't playing you through her?"

"Are you serious?"

"I'm dead serious," his brother yelled, coming to a stand. "Six weeks ago I scheduled a face-to-face meeting with him. He had to know what was up at that moment. His company was already in trouble and if Carrington were calling, Carrington wanted to buy. Mendoza's not a stupid man. He would have known that and he would have planned accordingly."

"He would have had no way of knowing I was going to be the one to meet with him instead," Jerald stated evenly.

Jackson shook his head. "No. But you're the money man at the company. You okay all the deals incoming and outgoing."

"You're the CEO," Jerald countered.

"It still falls on you. Good deal. Bad deal. You write that report. If your mind's been twisted by some—"

"Don't." Jerald interrupted him, stating the one word clearly, adamantly. "Don't call her out of her name. She's not involved with him like that. Not sexually and not on some kind of unsavory business arrangement. That's not what's going on here."

Jackson frowned but he did not speak right away. For endless moments the brothers simply stood there staring at each other.

"You in love with her?" Jackson asked him finally.

Jerald didn't hesitate with his reply. "I don't want her hurt. If I can get her to come and work for Carrington Enterprises she'll have the money she needs and tuition reimbursement. She won't need to work for Mendoza any longer."

Jackson lifted a brow. "That's not what I asked you."

"That's what I'm telling you," Jerald replied instantly. "That's what I plan to do for her. You close the deal with Carrington before the Feds snatch him up and we can't get him to sign that company away. That's what you can do, Jack. I'll take care of Hailey."

Jackson looked as if he were going to say something else but the knock at the door stopped him. Jerald went to open the door and was surprised this time to see who was standing on the other side.

"Mandi?" he asked when the intern smiled up at him.

"Hi, Mr. Carrington. We were all worried at the office when we heard about the incident. Noble said he would keep us posted when he left for the hospital but I wanted to see for myself that you were okay," she said, speaking in that very fast and excited tone she always had.

"Yes," Jerald spoke quickly before she could start again. "I'm fine. You didn't have to come all the way over here to see that for yourself."

"Oh, but I did," she said then stopped, biting her bottom lip, before smiling up at him nervously. "I mean, I figured you wouldn't want to come back to the office so I bought the work to you. I have all the Mendoza files and reports and today's stock rankings. I also have your white tea and your mug. I know how you prefer to use the same mug every day."

She'd attempted to hold up the small gift bag which most likely held his mug and tea and the two bags she'd slipped the files into, while holding a few other stacks of paper in her arms. Jerald reached out then, taking those stacks from her hands.

"Thank you, Mandi. Come on in," he told her.

Had she smiled a little brighter as she walked past him?

Jerald sighed inwardly as he caught a whiff of Mandi's very floral and extremely strong perfume. Closing the door behind him he watched as she made her way into the living room where Jackson was. She wore a short skirt—Mandi always wore short skirts—with a floral pattern on it, a wide black belt and a fitted white top. Her heels were a couple inches higher with a ton of sparkles that made them unprofessional and just a hint short of being gaudy.

"I guess we're working from home for the rest of the day," he heard Jack say when he returned to the living room.

"I guess so," was Jerald's bland reply.

Hailey stayed in her room for the rest of the afternoon and well into the night. After her run-in with Ronnel and his friend she'd locked the door and lay flat on her bed. When her thoughts and the events of the day had only made her head hurt more and her stomach roil in pain, she finally gave in to sleep as the only form of solitude she could find.

It was dark and quiet in her room when she awoke. Eerily quiet she figured after a few moments of lying there. Turning her head slowly she looked towards the window, memories from this morning flooding back into her mind. Someone had thrown a brick through the glass, a brick marked CHEATER. She'd seen the car, a black sedan, just like she'd told the police. No, she hadn't seen the license tag, nor had any faces been visible because the windows were tinted. But…

Hailey sat up in the center of her bed with a start. She had seen a hand and an arm, all clad in black. A black long sleeved shirt and gloved hand had appeared from the driver's side after the window had been wound down. Her heart was hammering in her chest as she closed her eyes tightly, trying desperately to see a face. That arm belonged to someone and if the window had been rolled down, why hadn't she been able to see that someone's face? Why only had she seen the arm, the hand, and the brick.

After a few more seconds of trying and not succeeding Hailey opened her eyes, looking towards the window once more. Sheer curtains hung from a couple inches away from the ceiling, down to the floor. They never kept the light out, which was Hailey's preference. Her bedroom back at Gram's house had room darkening curtains, ones her grandmother had lovingly hung when she was just a young girl and not a fan of bright lights.

Night had fallen while she'd slept but the sheer curtains still allowed a waning glow from the outside house lights to trickle inside. Hailey stood from the bed then, stretching her back, just as her stomach made an annoying twist. This probably wasn't anxiety or the buddings of fear that had come from seeing Ronnel staring at her the way he had…wait a minute, she thought, letting her arms fall back to her side.

Ronnel had sent her numerous text messages after the incident at the salon, but he hadn't come to see about them. He had not gotten into his personal SUV with his two bodyguards and his driver as he usually traveled, to come and make sure that his daughters were safe. Rhia had pointed that out the moment they arrived home.

And he'd called her his *mujer*. Friday night after he'd seen her coming out of the elevator with Jerald. He'd called her his woman. But she wasn't his woman.

Did that make her a CHEATER in his eyes?

No, she thought coming to a stand and shaking her head. No, this was all ridiculous. Ronnel Mendoza was not trying to train her to be his woman. That had been Jackson Carrington's assumption. She was only Ronnel's translator, only working for him for the summer.

Her stomach twisted again and this time Hailey realized she was hungry. And possibly delusional, given her most recent thoughts. With a sigh she headed to the bathroom where she planned to take a shower and then go downstairs to get something to eat, and possibly another pain pill because that damned headache was back.

For almost half an hour she'd stood in that stall with the water going from stinging hot to lukewarm as it cascaded down over her. Hailey had refused to think of Ronnel or all the bad things she'd heard about him anymore. Instead she'd lathered soap all over her body, then stood beneath the water as it washed free, loving the tingle of clean against her skin and the whisper of something else.

Arousal. She'd felt it the moment Jerald had walked into that salon this morning, as she had each time they were together. Today it had been more intense, an aching that centered in the pit of her stomach. That was what had angered her most about seeing him this morning, not the fact that he was still trying to get her to quit her job, but the notion that she would actually consider doing just that for this man.

She thrust her face beneath the water one last time, praying it would wash those foolish thoughts from her mind. No, she would not quit her job for Jerald Carrington, a man that wanted nothing from her but sex, that promised her nothing but...had he offered a job at his company? She was just shaking her head clear of that silly thought and switching off the music when she heard the sound.

It was a thump, as if something had fallen onto the floor in the other room. Stepping out of the shower quickly, Hailey grabbed the towel from the rack and wrapped it around her body. Her hair dripped, wet feet splashed water onto the floor as she headed towards the door. The moment she reached for the handle she heard another sound, something else hitting the floor, a lighter sound than before, but still...

Hailey yanked the door open and stepped onto the carpeted floor of her bedroom. And then she felt the breeze.

The window was open, those sheer curtains lifting and dancing as the cool evening breeze blew into the room. The lights were still off, at least until Hailey had moved to the table to turn on the lamp that sat there. But the lamp was gone.

Hurrying toward the main door of the room Hailey flipped the light switch there and watched as the bright golden glow illuminated the room. The lamp was on the floor. That's what she'd heard fall. Hailey gasped then as she saw her purse lying in the middle of the bed, emptied of all its contents. Her cell phone thrown on the floor.

Crossing the room quickly she picked up her belongings, setting them all on the bed beside her purse, surveying each item to make sure nothing was missing. It wasn't. But someone had definitely come in here and emptied everything out. Why? Still holding her cell phone in her hand Hailey thought she should call someone. The police maybe?

That window had been closed when she'd gone into the shower and her purse had been sitting on the nightstand where she'd put it when she came in earlier today. She'd gotten up to check the door and noted that it was still locked from when she'd come in here in a hurry to get away from Ronnel.

"No," she sighed. It couldn't have been him. He would have simply unlocked the door and come inside. This was his house after all.

Then it had to be someone else. Maybe the person that had thrown the brick. She switched on her phone, still not sure who she intended to call when a saved text message screen appeared. It had a message already drafted to be sent to her grandmother.

I'm so sorry Gram for messing everything up and for putting your life in danger.

She read that message over and over again before finally exiting the screen. Who would sneak in here to send a text message to her grandmother? And what type of danger was she in?

Very close to hyperventilating Hailey clenched her phone in her hands, closing her eyes in an attempt to calm her throbbing heart. When the phone vibrated in her hands she almost jumped off the bed. She answered it immediately, not bothering to look at the caller ID.

"Hey there," he said the moment she answered.

With her heart still pounding and her hands shaking, Hailey replied in as calm a voice as she could muster, "Hey yourself. Um, how are you feeling?"

"I should be asking you that question," he said.

Hailey looked around the room again, knowing there was no way that Jerald could know what had just happened, unless...

"What do you mean?" she asked him as she ran her shaking fingers through wet hair.

"You sound a little groggy, like maybe you just woke up," was his even reply. "I can't say that I blame you. I wanted to take a nap myself after those pain meds, but I ended up working from home."

He didn't know what had just happened. Hailey took a deep breath, letting it out slowly as he'd continued to talk. Jerald's voice had the effect of a comforting hug, circling around her as she sat on the edge of that bed, the lamp still on the floor, curtains still billowing in the breeze of the open window. She never thought she'd be happy to hear him calling her, but in this moment, she absolutely was.

"Well, a girl needs her beauty rest," she'd joked and got up to close that window.

"You're beautiful enough without any help," was his immediate reply.

Hailey did not respond to that. She did not know what to say.

"Let's go to dinner tonight," he said into the silence. "Do you like steak?"

She'd promised him dinner earlier today. Then, she'd figured she could come up with some reason not to at a later date. She had no idea he would call her on that agreement so soon. But to be perfectly honest, the last thing she wanted to do right now was turn him down. She wanted to get out of this house, away from the feeling that something here wasn't quite right. And who better to do that with than the man that had already warned her about staying here in the first place.

"My grandmother cooks the best steak and onions and gravy. She makes the fluffiest mashed potatoes and always serves green beans with the entrée. Can't have dinner without your vegetables, she always says." It was a memory that Hailey wasn't sure why she'd thought to share with him at this moment.

"That sounds delicious," Jerald replied.

"Yeah, and it's making me hungry. So you're on for dinner, Mr. Carrington," she said with a slow smile as she picked up the lamp and set it upright on the nightstand.

"Oh wait," she told him. "I don't think I have a ride."

She'd originally thought nothing had been taken from her purse. But the keys to the SUV were gone. With all that had happened earlier, she'd forgotten to hang the keys on the hook in the kitchen. Now, they were gone. The fear she'd wanted desperately to dismiss just a few minutes before about who could have come into her room while she was in the shower was renewed. Maybe one of the girls were looking for something. But why would the window be open and the door locked? Hailey was no detective. Hell, she'd never had to backtrack and try to remember faces and events, to come up with possible scenarios or to harbor the fear that was living and breathing inside of her now. No, none of this had ever been an issue for her when she was back east. Only now that she'd come to this place, to do a job she thought would save her and her grandmother's life, did things start to take a turn for the worst. She wondered if that was some sort of sign, fate somehow trying to warn her.

"Hailey?" Jerald called her name.

She had no idea how many times he'd done that or how long she'd been in her own thoughts, but she finally answered, "I'm here."

"I said I can pick you up."

"No!" she replied vehemently. "No, you can't drive up to the house. I'll meet you at the gate."

"Is everything alright, there?" he asked. "Mendoza didn't do anything to you when you came home earlier did he?"

Hailey was shaking her head when she realized Jerald couldn't see her. "No. Nothing happened. I've been in my room all afternoon." Which wasn't a lie. The part she neglected to mention was that she was certain someone else had been in this room also.

But at his mention of Mendoza, Malaya's words about him hurting people that made him angry had echoed in her mind once more.

"In an hour," she told Jerald. "I'll be at the front gate in an hour."

And she was. After calling to check on her grandmother, Hailey had dressed and moved as quietly as she could out of her bedroom. It was a little after seven and she'd been surprised that she'd slept so long. The girls would have had dinner already and would maybe be in the family room watching television. She had no idea where Ronnel was. There were no appointments on her calendar for meetings tonight but that didn't mean anything. That party last Friday had been a surprise and so had whoever he was talking to in the living room earlier today. With a shrug she told herself it was none of her business. Nothing that Jerald had said about Ronnel possibly being into human trafficking and being investigated by the FBI had anything to do with her and her reasons for being here. And if Ronnel wanted to continue to pay her to teach his daughters who already knew how to speak English, then she certainly would. What she would not do is give this man or anyone else control over her personal life.

She was going to dinner with Jerald, even if that meant she had to sneak out of this house to do so.

Hailey made it out of the house without incident, as if nobody gave a damn what she was doing or why. With a shrug she closed the front door behind her thinking there was no reason for any of them to care. She was just an employee after all. Her heels clicked on the cobblestones as she carefully moved through the courtyard and down the driveway. There were no vehicles parked out front. One of Ronnel's guards would have moved them into the garage as Ronnel did not like them blocking the view of the courtyard. The house had been quiet when she left which led her to believe the men he'd been meeting with earlier were also gone for the night.

Hailey had just walked through the fence door. It was located on the side of the huge gates that opened whenever a car was buzzed inside. The doorway was locked from the outside, but not the inside. Hailey did not have a key and wondered briefly how she would get back in. She would cross that bridge when she came to it, she thought, just as she began walking down the final slope leading to the open road. She stayed to the side so as to avoid any incoming cars and was immediately blinded by too bright headlights of a vehicle coming towards her.

Or at least she'd thought it was coming towards her. Instead it sped past with a screech of tires that reminded her of this morning and Hailey jumped back, a scream dying in her throat. The next car came up slowly, its lights a dull yellow as it came to a stop in front of her.

"You alright?" Jerald asked hopping quickly out of the car.

His hands were on her immediately and in seconds Hailey warmed. What was it about this guy, about his voice, his touch that always made her feel so good?

"I'm fine," she told him. "Just hungry."

Her smile was genuine as she looked up at him. She was hungry since breakfast had been her last meal today and with all the strange things that had happened to her today, she was happy to see him. The one person that had made her feel…no, she wasn't going to go that far. She liked being with Jerald, or rather liked having sex with him. Tonight would be their first time actually being together.

"Then I should definitely hurry up and feed you," he said, walking her around to the passenger side of his car.

"Yes," she said as he opened the door and then stood close to her. "You should definitely do that."

For a few quiet seconds they stood just as they had in the hospital, Jerald looking down to her, and she looking up at him. Both of them wondering what the hell was going on between them. Neither of them willing to take the chance of answering.

Jerald used his napkin to wipe his mouth after he'd chewed his last bite of steak. He reached for his glass and took a sip of his wine as Hailey spoke.

"I promised my grandfather that I would take care of my grandmother and that I would finish school," she said with a shrug as if it didn't mean as much to her as he suspected it really did.

"I'll be the first in the family to have a college degree, and from Brown, no less. They'll be so proud," she continued, letting her hands fall into her lap.

They'd been talking lightly throughout dinner, him telling her about his brothers and his parents, about their business and his sisters-in-law. Jerald had never talked to a woman about his family before. He'd never wanted to. But when Hailey asked, he hadn't been able to deny her.

"You should be proud," he told her. "It takes a lot of dedication to finish school, especially under your circumstances."

She nodded, brushing a curly tuft of hair behind her ear. "My circumstances being that I don't have enough money for tuition." She gave a little chuckle. "You'd be surprised how many people do not have the money to go to school, Jerald."

"No," he told her honestly. "I wouldn't be. I know that college is expensive and I know that it costs too much for the average teenager to even consider going. That's why we offer tuition reimbursement for all our employees and their immediate family. Carrington Enterprises also funds a scholarship at UCLA and Columbia where my grandfather and my father attended."

She was shocked, he could tell by the way her eyes widened a bit.

"You didn't think we could do anything for anyone else because we have money," he said and couldn't help frowning at her.

"No," she told him. "I'll be perfectly honest when I tell you that I didn't think that much about your family or your business. I couldn't afford to."

"You have to understand that for the last five years all I've been focused on is making enough money to help my grandmother with her bills and to pay for school, one semester at a time. I can't think about how the younger girls on campus are staring at me because I'm not full-time and instead of hanging with them in study hall or going to parties, I'm always hurrying off campus to get to my apartment that only holds a mattress, a table and a chair because that's all I need while I'm in school."

Hailey continued, "So no, I didn't think about the Carringtons or their money or their efforts to give back to the community. I guess that makes me selfish or single-minded."

Jerald could only stare at her. "It makes you motivated," he told her honestly.

"How did you end up in Turks and Caicos if you barely had money to go to school?" he asked a question that had been nagging him since Jackson had left his apartment earlier today.

His brother had planted the seed that Mendoza could have been using Hailey to get at him all along. Jerald didn't agree. But he did have questions.

"I have Rhia and Malaya to thank for that," she replied after taking another sip of her wine. "They'd begged their father for a vacation and when he asked where they wanted to go Rhia said Turks and Caicos. He gives them whatever they want and believe me they know it. So I went on the vacation with them. Me and their nanny."

"And you were just sitting on the beach in the middle of the night?" he asked, recalling the moment.

"I'd never been to a place like that before. It was gorgeous. I wanted a minute alone to enjoy it, without the chatter of two very privileged and just a tad obnoxious girls that spoke perfect English. I waited until they all went to sleep before I came out to the beach. I walked into that warm Caribbean water and thought better of swimming out there at night alone. So I ended up sitting on the beach. Then you came along."

She licked her lips after saying that, as if she'd been recalling what happened after he'd found her on the beach as well. The sight of her sitting there, her legs partially spread had drawn him instantly to her. Full breasts and long legs, they'd always been his preference. But it was when she'd looked up at him, her hazel eyes staring back at him with such honesty and simplicity that had taken his breath away. Seconds later he'd thought she had to be very experienced to pull that off. Now, he knew it wasn't experience at all. Hailey was the most genuine female he'd ever met.

"You thought I worked for someplace called The Corporation. What's that? An escort service of some kind? Did you get your money back after I told you I didn't work there? Because I know you called to verify my story," she said pointedly.

Jerald had no intention of lying to her. He signaled the waiter for another drink for both of them and emptied his glass before replying.

"I did check," he replied. "The Corporation is a sex club. It's a place that provides any and every thing a person could crave sexually."

He'd expected her to flinch, but she did not. Instead, she'd arched an eyebrow and asked, "You frequent this place often?"

"I only deal with professional women," was his quick response. It might have been too quick, he thought when her other brow raised and she actually looked, disappointed.

"So you expected me to go up to your room with you because you'd already paid for it. Not because I wanted to, or because you actually wanted me. It was a business deal."

"It was," he replied honestly. "In the beginning. Then it changed."

"When?" she asked, tilting her head as if she thought he was going to lie.

He wasn't because that wasn't his style. He did not lie to women because he did not want them to lie to him. If what Hailey thought about him as a man had begun to matter to Jerald more than what anyone else had ever thought of him before, then he would deal with that. But he would not lie to her.

"After I returned home I knew there had been something different about you. I didn't expect to see you again so I tried to brush that feeling off as the scenery or the summer heat. Then you showed up at that meeting and I knew. You were different and I liked that. I liked it a lot."

Their new drinks arrived and Hailey picked up her glass first. She took a long, slow sip, her gaze locked with his.

"What else do you like, Jerald? When you book these professional women, what else do you like them to do? I'm sure I didn't do everything you would have paid for."

She'd set her glass down and was now rubbing the tip of her finger up and down the stem. Jerald's dick had come quickly to attention as he imagined her running those fingers up and down his length, the way she did after she'd slipped a condom on him.

"Why do you want to know?" he asked.

"I'm curious," was her slow reply.

Jerald waited a beat. No, he waited two while he contemplating his next words. She was different, he'd admitted that already. She did not work for The Corporation, had no idea a place like that had even existed. And yet…she was curious.

"Drink your wine," he told her. "And come with me."

CHAPTER 8

Jerald helped her out of the car, lacing his fingers with hers. For a second he looked down at their clasped hands, his skin touching hers. It wasn't sexual even though during the ride he'd definitely been thinking about slipping that simple, yet overwhelmingly sexy, black dress off her body. He would go slowly this time, he told himself again. Slow enough to savor every second, to taste every inch, touch every crevice. It wasn't like he needed the memory since the camera was already set up in his bedroom. At one time, he'd wondered why he'd purchased two sets of camera equipment—one for his room at The Corporation and the other for his home—when he'd never planned to have a woman in his personal space. Now, he smiled to himself knowing it was there and in place for when he returned tonight with Hailey. He just wanted to show her something first.

"Why do you do that?" Hailey asked him.

Jerald looked up, dragging his gaze away from their joined hands to stare into her pretty face.

"Give me orders," she replied. "'Come up to my room.' 'Come with me.' 'Quit your job.' Is it because of our age difference? Do you have some type of daddy complex?"

She'd been smiling as she talked, but Jerald knew she was serious. He hadn't given a lot of thought to the fact that there were ten years between them. When he spoke to her, he simply said what came to his mind. The same things he said to the other women he dealt with. Only what he hadn't realized, or what he'd wanted to continuously tell himself didn't matter, was that Hailey was not like those other women. The mere fact that she'd asked him that question in the first place had cemented that in his mind.

"It's a habit," he told her. "I have a lot of them. My family would attribute them to the OCD diagnosis I've had since I was ten years old. I just call them my habits." He shrugged then, wondering why he'd said so much. A simple "I don't know" or "does it bother you?" would have either ended this line of conversation or taken it in another direction, away from him. It's what he would have normally done with a woman, to take the focus from him and put it on the sex they were about to have.

He looked down at his hand entwined with Hailey's once more and then asked, "Does it bother you?"

"It did," she began. "At first."

His head jerked up and their gazes met once more. "And now?"

"It's growing on me," she replied, smiling at him again. "I think you're growing on me, Jerald."

"That's interesting," he said rubbing his thumb along the back of her hand. "Very interesting."

They'd walked a few steps, crossing the level of the garage where he was licensed to park. He'd just swiped his membership card to access the elevator when her next question surfaced. Jerald figured this was just the beginning of their question and answer session for tonight. Once she was inside, Hailey would certainly have more and he would be happy to answer them.

"Where are you taking me?" she asked. "This place looks really official. I hope it doesn't have anything to do with Ronnel and his business. That's not something I want to get involved in, Jerald. Especially if you and your brother are right about what you've said."

The elevator door opened and they stepped inside. It did not look like an ordinary elevator, Jerald knew. The way

Hailey was looking around as Jerald pressed the button for the floor they wanted, said she was thinking the same thing.

"We're not going to talk about Mendoza again. I think you're beginning to realize that my warnings are well founded," he told her.

"I'm beginning to realize something," she mumbled rubbing her hand over the brass arm railing along the wall of the compartment.

Behind the railing was rich cherry wood paneling, buffed and glossed to perfection and the floor was covered in a plush forest green carpet, giving the compartment a warm and stately appearance.

"That I was right and you were wrong?" he asked.

It was her turn to look up at him sharply, as if his words had sparked something inside of her.

"No. That people aren't always what they seem," she told him.

They stared at each other for the next few seconds, him wondering whether or not she was including him in those "people" and her, probably wondering what would happen next. When the elevator door opened and he took her hand in his once more, he wanted to tell her that she had no idea. None at all.

"In answer to your question," Jerald said instead, as he led her off the elevator. "This is The Corporation."

There were Corporation facilities all over the world. So far, in the time that he'd known about this place, he'd had the chance to visit only four—New York, Miami, and Turks and Caicos—including his home locale in Beverly Hills. Each facility had a different themed décor. All of which were stately and very exquisitely done. Jerald knew the layout of the Beverly Hills location very well. It had an old law firm feel with its heavy dark oak furniture, rich mahogany painted walls and plush forest green carpet. From one room to the next, some separated by heavy marble columns, others by dark brown shutter doors, there was an air of money and privilege thickly layered over the foundation of sexual pleasure and fantasies.

It smelled of new leather throughout the facility, contracted employees dressed in black suits, with staff dressed in white pants and shirts and red ties—males and females—moving throughout unobtrusively. Jerald recognized some of the faces he saw as they stood near the bank of elevators. However, he'd never held lengthy conversations with any of them because that wasn't what he'd come here for.

The first floor of The Corporation was set up like one big lounge, each room fitted with deep cushioned leather chairs, sturdy wooden side tables, Persian rug overlays and some with floor to ceiling windows looking out over the city of the rich and famous. Drinks were provided to each member without the necessity of the member placing an order. The staff at The Corporation had an extensive file on each of their members, they knew what they liked, what they disliked and what they would probably pay extra for, before the member even stepped through the door.

Tonight, Hailey was his guest. She had not been officially vetted by The Corporation staff and as such would need to be signed in. Jerald began walking towards the front desk, which looked more like a bar, complete with the mirrored background and glass shelves stacked with crystal clear glasses and bottles of top shelf liquor.

He recognized the receptionist working tonight. She normally sat at the first floor entrance of the club. Her name was Cheyenne.

"Good evening," Jerald said to Cheyenne as they approached. "I have a guest with me tonight."

"No problem, Mr. Carrington. I'll just need to see her identification card and get your signature on the log," Cheyenne replied brightly.

"Here's your drink, Mr. Carrington," a staff member came up beside him holding a tray with a glass of his preferred vodka on the rocks. "Is there something special I can get your guest?"

Hailey looked up then after handing her ID card to Cheyenne. "I'll have what he's having," she replied.

Jerald nodded to the staff member as she had looked to him again for confirmation.

"Because I'm just a guest I can't order my own drink?" she asked him when they walked away from Cheyenne.

She was carrying her own vodka on the rocks in one hand, her other arm twined through his.

"It's your first time here. They'll develop a profile for you from this point on. So if I bring you back they'll automatically have a vodka on the rocks for you. If there's something different you want, they'll get it and add that to your profile as well."

"But only if I'm with you?"

Jerald paused. "This is a member's only club, Hailey. You can either purchase a membership, which is not cheap by any stretch, or you can come in as a guest. There are rules and protocols, and waiting periods for special privileges," he said.

"But above all else," he continued. "There is pleasure."

She blinked before taking a sip of her drink and Jerald continued walking. There were several different rooms on this floor, all separated by archways and columns. Upstairs housed the private rooms and suites. The play rooms were on the floor below. He did not want to play with Hailey tonight. His goal was to simply show her where he thought she'd worked. If that was giving her a more personal glimpse of the man he was, well, that wasn't his intention. He was only slightly surprised to realize he wasn't totally opposed to that either.

"You're a member of this club," she asked when they crossed the entire floor and were near the windows to the back of the building.

Booths lined the far wall, more oak with red felt covering on the benches and glossy table tops which held the member's drink and/or their entertainment. Tonight, there were two men sitting in one booth and one woman between them. Another man sat in a booth, watching and…playing, Jerald surmised from the fact that while his drink was on the table, his hands were not. And following the man's gaze straight across the room was a woman, her skirt hiked up so high the cheeks of her ass were visible. So were the man's hands that were gripping them.

"Yes. I am," was his simple response.

Jerald walked Hailey to another side of the room where patio doors were covered with red brocade drapes. Members that came to this room could have privacy, or not. It was their choice.

Lined in front of the patio doors were three chaise lounges covered in black velour and made to accommodate two, or possibly three depending on the position. He extended his hand signaling her to take a seat. She did even though she looked like she wasn't certain this was a good idea. He sat at the head of the lounge, bringing his glass to his lips to take a swallow before speaking again.

"This is easier than dating," he said, still feeling the need to tell her things about himself—everything about himself to be exact.

They weren't a couple, he reminded himself. Bringing her here, answering her questions honestly, none of that meant they were committed to each other in any way. He simply wanted to help her. Did he also want to continue sleeping with her? Yes. But one thing did not necessarily have anything to do with the other.

"It's hiding," was her slow reply.

Across the room both men had a palm on that woman's breasts, squeezing and kneading as they leaned in to whisper something in her ear.

"You call that hiding? We can see them and they know it," he told her before taking another drink from his glass. "They're going to fuck her right there in that booth, both of them. And if we sit here long enough, we can watch. I don't think they're hiding anything."

"They're hiding their true selves," she countered. "Who really wants to sit in a dark club and have sex while strangers watch? Someone who doesn't want anyone to see the real person they are. Everyone in here is hiding because they're members to a secret club."

"What if they think the world won't understand their urges? Is it their fault then that this is what they have to resort to so that they won't be judged?" he asked.

"Nobody has the right to judge another person."

Jerald shook his head. "They don't need the right to do it, Hailey. They just do."

"Is that why you come here, so nobody will judge you for wanting to have anonymous sex? Or is it something more, Jerald?"

He emptied his glass then, holding it tightly in his hands as he continued to watch the two men who had now undone the front of the woman's blouse. They were each sucking her small breasts, as if their very life depended on it.

"I like my lifestyle," he told her. "Do you like yours?"

"I like deciding that I'll sleep with a guy because I want to and not because I'm being paid to," she snapped.

She didn't bother with her drink again, but set it down on the floor close to her feet.

"Do you want to leave?" he asked. "Or do you want to see what other pleasures can be had here?"

"I'm not into watching others," she replied primly.

Jerald turned to her then, touching a palm to her knee that had been bouncing rhythmically since they'd sat down. "And yet you haven't turned away from them once," he said, lowering his voice as he leaned closer to her.

"This is the part you don't want anyone to see or know about. The part where watching those mean suck on her breasts makes you want to reach up and touch your own nipples. To pull on them until they sting and burn the way you believe hers feel as each one of those men suckle and close their teeth around hers."

He moved back further in the chair, touching his arms to her shoulders as he pulled her gently back with him. "From the moment you sat down you've been tapping your foot on the floor, your knee moving up and down in succession. Nervous energy," he told her as he returned his hand to the knee he was referring to. "Or sexual energy?"

"I've seen porn flicks before, Jerald. This is nothing new," she said, clearing her throat afterwards and shifting to adjust her dress and herself on the chair beside him.

"This isn't a flick. It's live, up front and personal. The energy in this room is contagious. It releases all inhibitions."

"It gives permission to something that might otherwise be scrutinized," she said. "I get what you're saying but that doesn't mean I want to be a part of it."

Jerald paused a second. What he was thinking and considering was something he'd never entertained before. He was private and so were his meetings with the employees of The Corporation. Hell, he doubted anyone other than the staff actually knew his name. And yet tonight, things were changing.

The hand on her knee moved upward, until he was touching her inner thigh, her dress hiking up with the movement.

"Then tell me to stop," he told her. "Tell me to stop and that you want to leave and I'll get up and take you home."

He looked into her eyes then, saw the golden flecks just seconds before they darkened with her growing desire. She opened her mouth to speak, but instead licked her tongue along her bottom lip. He moved his hands again, until it was between her legs following the heat emanating from her center. His fingers touched the silky fabric of her underwear.

"I never thought much about women's underwear until you," he whispered, his fingers pushing past the fabric to touch the warm folds of her pussy. "Now, I want to go out and buy you a lifetime supply of thongs and matching bras. If only so that I can rip them off whenever I feel like it. To fuck you whenever I feel the need."

"You're not scaring me," she told him, her breath catching slightly the moment the pad of his finger moved over her clit.

"Oh no," he said with a deep, low chuckle. "I'm not trying to scare you, Hailey. Just please you."

He circled his finger over her clit once more, his body tingling all over at the intoxicating sensation of touching the tightened bud.

"Keep watching them," he whispered as he dipped his head lower, his teeth nipping the line of her jaw.

"Watch as one of them continues to suck her breasts and the other reaches low to finger her," he instructed.

His kisses went lower, his tongue tracing a line along her jaw then down her neck. The dress she wore tonight was modest enough with its button front and tightly cinched hot pink belt. She could have been going to any casual dinner, with any man that had been lucky enough to ask her out. But she was with him, in this place that promised sexual pleasure. Jerald had no qualms about taking that pleasure, about pushing the limits between them, about having her completely. None at all.

Using his mouth he undid one of those damned buttons so that the breasts that the dress was barely containing were just about free. Licking between the crevice of her mounds, Jerald pushed one finger, then a second, into her hot pussy. She was so wet and so hungry for him, sucking his fingers in immediately and arching her back so he could have greater access to her breasts. And she was watching. He was certain that she was still watching the threesome across the room.

He thrust deeper, raking his teeth over the plump mounds of her breasts as she began to moan. He tore his mouth away from her long enough to say, "Tell me what they're doing now."

She sucked in a deep breath, her legs trembling. For a moment she didn't speak, warring with whether or not she should, he surmised.

"It's okay Hailey. They want you to watch. They want you to see it all," Jerald said. He licked the soft skin of her breast then sucked that spot before saying, "Tell me sweetheart. Tell me what they're doing to her."

"She's on his lap now," Hailey said whispering slightly when he pumped his fingers inside her faster.

"She's facing forward so that the other guy can continue sucking her breasts. I think the other guy is inside her, pumping...into...her. He's pumping her fast and hard just...like..." she ended on a sigh as Jerald circled his fingers inside her pussy.

"Is she enjoying it?" he asked, his dick so stiff it was becoming harder and harder to think.

How long had he wanted this feeling? How many nights had he laid in his bed during rehab and craved this exact feeling? And no matter how many women, or how many videos, he'd never accomplished it. Not until Hailey.

"Yes," she muttered. "Yes, she's loving every minute of...it. It's so good. So damn, good."

To her and the other woman, Jerald presumed.

"Would you love it if I fucked you right here?" he asked, his voice gruff with desire. "Right here on this chair for all to see...I could...spread your legs and plunge my dick deep inside of you. They would see us and they would enjoy it too."

No, Jerald thought seconds after he'd spoken. That's not what he wanted at all. He went completely still as he realized he could not do that. He did not want anyone seeing him fuck her, seeing her enjoy him and find her own pleasure. That was all for him. Hailey was all for him.

He pulled away from her, coming to a stand. Extending his hand to her he said, "Come with—" He paused then and continued to stare at her and took a deep breath before starting again. "Please come with me, Hailey. I need to have you right now, but not here, not like this."

She'd closed her legs and fixed the button on her dress before taking his hand and standing.

"It's always because I want to," she said looking directly at him. "There's no other reason, Jerald. Not money or circumstances or anything else you might think."

He was shaking his head as he linked his fingers with hers. "Because you want to, I understand," he told her, believing those words more than he'd believed anything in a long time.

Hailey wanted to be with him and he wanted her. He wanted all of her.

He'd paused only a second to push those thick brocade drapes away from where he knew the handle of the patio door was. Unlocking it, he pushed the door open and moved until he was standing outside and so was she. It was dark out here, no overhead lighting at all. There were two chairs at the far end but Jerald had no intention of going there.

Instead, he pushed Hailey until her back was to the wall, his body covering her completely so that if by some chance someone in the building across from them had binoculars and planned for some entertainment tonight, they wouldn't see her.

"I don't know why I have to have you," he muttered while using a hand to undo his pants, his zipper and pulling his erection free. "Every damned time."

She'd pushed his hand away, gripping his thick length in her hands and stroking. "Me either," she replied. "I've never been this way with anyone before. Never."

"Good," Jerald groaned and he picked her up in his arms aiming his length at her center. "Let me in, Hailey. Just me. Just let me in."

And she did, keeping her hands between them but moving this time to ease that piece of silk covering her pussy to the side so that the head of his dick could slip right in.

They both groaned on contact as she wrapped her legs tightly around his waist and her arms around his neck. Jerald pulled out slowly then thrust back in, loving the feel of her warm honey coating his raw dick. Closing his eyes to the pleasure Jerald heard her whispering his name as she dropped light kisses along his cheek, until coming to his lips.

"I don't know what this is," she whispered. "But I'm beginning to like it…a lot. I'm beginning to…want…you…a lot."

"You want me, you can have me. And I can have you," he said without a second's thought. His dick moving in and out of her with a practiced ease, his chest heaving with the breaths it was taking to keep them standing upright.

She flexed her hips, meeting him stroke for stroke until they were both panting and moaning, their release taking them simultaneously and with more force than he figured either of them could have anticipated.

They used Jerald's room upstairs to get cleaned up before Hailey admitted she should probably return to the Mendoza house.

"I don't like you staying there," Jerald said while they stood at the door.

He hadn't left her this time, a fact that was ringing like victory bells in her head since the moment he'd pulled out of her and suggested they come up to his room. There'd been something different about their joining tonight. No, not just that it was the first time she'd ever had sex outside, or her first trip to a sex club. As monumental as those two things were, they didn't compare to what had transpired between her and Jerald. He'd seemed different, more open, more right there in the moment with her than he'd been the other times they'd been together. And she'd been silly enough to admit to him that she wanted him, that she couldn't help but always want him.

Hailey did not consider herself a fool. She knew their differences—they were worlds apart and not just in actual distance between L.A. and Virginia. He was rich and influential and she was struggling to finish school and take care of her ailing grandmother. It's a wonder their paths had ever crossed. Yet, here they were.

"It's my job," she told him.

"Because you need to help your grandmother. I understand that, Hailey. I really do. But you don't have to do this. The internship at my company is a paid one. You'll get a bi-weekly check. And the tuition reimbursement forms will be enough to get you registered for the semester. We have contracts that work out special financial arrangement with all of the universities throughout the United States. Then, once your grades are in, the school can send the bill directly to us and we'll pay it."

Hailey had looked away from him as he explained his offer once more. It was too good to be true, just as the offer from Mendoza had been. She needed to be smarter this time, especially since she was starting to believe she was in over her head with Mendoza.

When Jerald touched a finger to her chin, tilting her head up so she was once again staring into his eyes, all thoughts of precaution and hesitation fled from her mind.

"It's not just school, Jerald. And my grandmother doesn't just have bills." She inhaled deeply and figured there really was no purpose in holding this back from him. "My grandmother has cancer. She's going to need to undergo surgery and then treatment. And those asbestos lawyers don't always deliver what they promise. Mendoza is offering me so much."

Jerald shook his head. "No. He's not offering you enough. Not enough to put your life at risk. You and your grandmother will get health care insurance through my company. You'll both be taken care of."

"For how long?" she asked him. "As long as I continue to sleep with you and you with me? What kind of arrangement is this you're offering me, Jerald?"

He grew quiet then. The sound, or lack thereof, hitting her like a punch to the gut.

"Look, I appreciate your offer. And I want you to know that I'm going to think about it and my arrangement with Mendoza very carefully," she said.

It was true, she did plan to think about both offers and to figure out a way to do something else on her own. She could not stay in L.A. and be Jerald's very well paid mistress any more than she could continue to work for Mendoza and wonder what was going to happen to her next.

"I want to help you," he told her again. He kept saying that as if it were enough, for him at least.

Hailey nodded. "I know you do and that's very commendable of you. But I think I'm starting to realize that I can do a better job of helping myself, without any strings attached. I'll figure this out, Jerald. There's no need for you to worry about it any longer."

Hailey walked out of the room then, knowing that he would follow her but hoping this would end the conversation. He had to drive her back to the Mendoza estate and she had to tiptoe inside. This was not the way her summer was supposed to play out. It wasn't the life her grandparents would want her to lead, even if it was helping to pay their bills.

They'd just stepped out of the elevator, Jerald holding her hand once more when Hailey felt something strange. It was as if the hairs on the back of her neck stood up, a weird feeling that had her shivering in the coolness of the garage.

"You okay?" Jerald asked as the continued to move to where he'd parked his car.

"Yes," she began, looking around behind her. "I'm fi—"

Her words were cut off by the sound of a car door and footsteps. She stopped then, turning completely around to see where the footsteps were coming from, or more likely where they were leading. That's when she saw him.

The man that had been talking to Ronnel earlier today. If his tall, bulky build hadn't been the giveaway, that nasty scar on his arm was. She gasped and felt Jerald's arms come up around her.

"What is it? Do you know that guy?"

Hailey shook her head. "No. I…um, I mean yes."

The man had opened a car door and slipped inside then and before she could say another word to Jerald he'd started the car and pulled out of the spot, tires screeching loudly. If she and Jerald hadn't moved out of the way, the dark sedan would have run them down.

As it was, Jerald had acted quickly, once again covering her body with his as he fell to the ground and rolled out of the car's way.

"I keep ending up in your arms," Hailey said, heart beating wildly as she lay on the cement looking up at him.

He smiled down at her then. "I'm not complaining."

No, he wasn't, Hailey thought. But he wasn't making any promises to her either. Not that they could be together and then he could help her. That offer wasn't going to come, not from a man like Jerald Carrington and especially not for her.

"Can I get up now?" she asked and attempted to move.

But Jerald stood first and then reached to help her up. "Did you know that guy?" he asked her again.

"I thought…um, I thought he looked familiar," she told him.

"Familiar from where?"

Hailey shrugged, not sure she should tell Jerald more of what had happened at Ronnel's house. They were doing business together and even if Ronnel was probably a mean SOB, there were still the girls to consider. What would happen to Rhia & Malaya if their father's business was taken?

"I don't know," she said shaking her head. "I could have been wrong."

But she knew she wasn't. That guy had been here, at this private sex club at the same time that she was. It was no coincidence she knew, and that gave her even more cause to worry about Ronnel.

"You're shaking," Jerald said. "If you didn't know him, then why are you shaking?"

"Because earlier today a brick was thrown at me and now a car just tried to run me down. I think I have a right to shake at this point," she said vehemently.

Jerald looked at her as if he could relate to what she was saying. Sure, he could. He'd been with her on both occasions.

"I'd just like to get back to the house so I can get some rest."

"You cannot continue to stay there," Jerald told her. "We can work out the details of my offer to you, but please, Hailey. Please, just tell me you'll check into a hotel. I'll pay for it if that's a problem. But you need to get out of Mendoza's house."

He sounded adamant, almost to the point that Hailey thought he might not even take her back to Ronnel's place.

"You're right," she agreed, because he was. Especially after having just seen that man. Was Ronnel having her followed? Did he really believe she was cheating on him with Jerald? Whatever the answer to those questions, they weren't right. None of this was what she'd wanted to happen when she came here. So, Hailey had decided in those few moments, she would leave. She would go back to Ronnel's pack her bags and quit the job that was supposed to be her salvation. She had no other choice.

"I'm not going to stay there," she told Jerald and watched as he breathed a sigh of relief. "But I'll take care of my arrangements."

He looked like he wanted to frown, but instead said, "That's fine. For now."

Jerald was no fool.

Lacking experience when it came to committing to women, or even contemplating doing so, but he was no fool.

Hailey had definitely recognized that man and since she didn't want to tell him from where, Jerald had no choice but to find out on his own. After he'd dropped her off and stood at the gate watching until he could no longer see her, he'd climbed back in his car and pulled out his phone.

First, he called the front desk at The Corporation and asked which member had the license plate that matched the one on that sedan he'd memorized just before being almost run down. Cheyenne promised to have someone from the corporate office contact him tomorrow. He'd told her about the almost accident to give her some background on why he was asking for the information. As expected, the woman had been immediately concerned. So would the executives of The Corporation. No way were they going to have one member inflicting violence on another, especially not on a Carrington. They would want to get to the bottom of this as soon as possible, and that was fine with Jerald.

His next call had been to D&D Investigations where once again, he'd reiterated tonight's events and added in today's earlier adventures.

The conversation was a long one filled with Jerald giving details and the man on the other end mostly saying, "I see" and "Really now". Jerald was only mildly concerned when he was about to hang up and the man said, "I'll be there first thing in the morning."

So he was coming, not Trent Donovan. Trent had always been their contact at D&D. Jerald had no idea who this Devlin Bonner was, but figured he would find out soon.

Minutes after ending the call Jerald walked down the hall towards his penthouse. Unlocking the door he let himself in and that's when he felt it. Something was off.

Moving to the sofa table, Jerald opened a drawer slowly. He removed the gun—a 9mm that he'd been licensed to carry two years ago when a madman was threatening Jason and Celise. Releasing the safety Jerald continued to walk throughout the first floor of his place, looking for the cause of this unsettled feeling.

He found nothing.

Taking the steps slowly he continued to look throughout the rooms upstairs, the guest bathrooms and the home office he used. When he entered his bedroom the sense of dread grew and Jerald hastily turned on the lights. After checking the bathroom and deducing that there was no one here, he continued to look around. He paused when he saw the open cabinet. It was tall, dark cherry wood with gold handles on each door and drawer. It sat in the far corner of his bedroom, nearest the windows, and the top front door was opened.

Jerald moved slowly toward the cabinet, as if he thought an intruder could actually hide in this small space. But that wasn't what had concerned him. Reaching out he pulled the door all the way open and cursed, long and fluently.

This was the cabinet where he'd kept his videos. All of them were gone. Every escapade he'd had with a woman in his room at The Corporation were gone. On another curse he opened the lower draw only to feel like the entire room was spinning around him when he realized the video of him and Hailey in Turks and Caicos was also gone.

With tense strides Jerald moved to the stand beneath his television, where his home entertainment center was housed. He pressed the power button on the DVD player, then the eject and fell to his knees with relief that the video of Hailey in his bedroom was still there. Saved by the fact that he'd once again watched it this morning when he'd awakened.

The other videos hadn't been so lucky. And when Jerald found out who had broken into his home to steal what belonged to him, they weren't going to consider themselves lucky either. Not by a fucking longshot!

THE ONE

Betrayal left a sour taste in my mouth.

Again.

They were fucking. On the beach. In his house. At the club. He was inside of her and I was about to lose my everlasting mind!

I wanted to scream until my voice was gone, to lash out…again…but this time with more than a brick and a text message that I didn't get the chance to send.

This had to stop!

I had to stop it, before it was too late.

CHAPTER 9

Hailey's body hummed with satisfaction. She hugged the pillow so tight she could swear strong arms were hugging her right back.

You want me, you can have me.

Jerald's words had played over and over in her mind throughout the night until she'd finally fallen into a comfortable sleep. And then she'd dreamed of him, his touch, his kiss, the way he moved inside of her so deep that once again she felt like they were joined and as if they were meant to be together.

Yes, she wanted him. Oh, how she wanted that man. In the confines of her bedroom she could admit that to herself. Sure, she'd told him but she wasn't certain he'd grasped the totality of that admission. In all her life, Hailey had only ever wanted to please and take care of her grandparents the way they had her. School and a career were reachable goals in her mind, they were the tangible part of life she could obtain. While love and happiness through a committed relationship had not been in the forefront, because it could be lost. The way she'd lost her parents and her grandfather.

Tonight, however, Hailey had felt differently. She'd not only opened her mind to the sex club but she'd felt herself opening her heart to a guy that she had no idea whether or not he wanted to be there in the first place. Her re-entrance into Ronnel's house had been seamless as she felt like she was practically floating through the courtyard and up the stairs to her room. It was strange, considering all that had happened just before she'd left Jerald. Hell, all that had occurred since she'd met Jerald.

Her mind, for whatever reason, chose to hang on to the positive, to a dream she'd never dared give the time of day. That dream had blurred from one scene to the next, from their heated sexual stint on the balcony to a beautiful house in Beverly Hills, with a sparkling pool and white roses strewn all over the ground. A path of roses led to a spread of white chairs, a white runner stretching between them to meet an archway covered in more roses and Jerald standing there waiting for her.

"He's The One," Pops said from beside her. Arthur wore a white tuxedo with tails, complete with a top hat that made him look like royalty as he stood with his arm bent, lifted and waiting for her.

"He is," she told him before lacing her arm through his and allowing him to walk her down that runner. "He is The One."

There were people in those white chairs, faces that were not clear but whose happiness emanated throughout the air with each step she took. She wore white, the silk material brushing softly against her body and the sun was warm across her face. But she wasn't, she was instead, happier than she'd ever been.

At the altar, a minister spoke in a muttered voice and Jerald lifted the veil from her face, leaning in to kiss her to the sound of applause from all those faceless guests. It was magical and whimsical and everything her grandparents had always told her falling in love and marrying The One would be.

And then there was a noise and Hailey gasped, turning away from the white and the perfect, to face the dark and the evil. With a whimper she tossed and turned in the bed, this time landing flat on her back. The serene feeling of wafting through dreamland had dissipated, leaving her with a sudden urge to run. To get up from this bed, pack her bags and run long and far.

When her heart began to pound at the thought, Hailey pulled herself from sleeping, feeling as if her body were being tugged back into that darkness, that abyss of fear she'd been trying her best to ignore. But when her eyes finally opened, when they'd adjusted to the dimly lit room, she could only gasp at what part of the dream had followed her through to reality.

"You smile when you sleep," Ronnel said from where he stood at the foot of her bed. "You dream of fucking him."

It was clear from the brisk and stilted tone of his voice that he was angry and Hailey grabbed the sheet to her chest as she came to a sitting position in the center of the bed. "What the hell are you doing in here?"

"It is my house," he replied as if that fact should have been a given and acceptable excuse. His hands were fisted at his sides, another one of his famous scarves wrapped around his neck while his shirt was only half buttoned.

"I gave you what you wanted and still you betray me," he continued, disappointment obvious and heavy in his voice.

Her instincts were clear and screaming loudly in her head. This wasn't a dream. This man—this clearly unstable man—was standing in her room in the middle of the night. He had been standing there for who knew how long, doing what she could only surmise as being weird and on some level demented.

Hailey should get off this bed. She was a sitting duck here but her nightgown was so short the last thing she wanted was to get up and have him seeing her half nude. Hailey had no idea what was going to happen next or why this lunatic was in her room ranting as if he owned her on some level. But she was definitely through with this roller coaster ride, there was no more denying that fact.

"How could I betray you? I did my job the way I was supposed to," she said using every bit of strength she had to remain calm in the midst of this uncertain situation.

"I tell you not to see him. You fuck him in that nasty club, for all the people to see," he spoke as if he were stating simple truths. In seconds he followed up with, "*Kalapating mababa ang lipad!*"

Hailey jumped in shock. She couldn't help it. She'd never heard him speak this way before and certainly had never had anyone call her what he had—a slut. That reaction was only temporary, to be replaced quickly by her own bit of outrage. She pushed back the covers and jumped out of the bed. "You bastard! I asked for a job and you gave me one. I've done everything I was supposed to do. If you thought there was something else going on that was your fault. Not mine!"

"You are right," he said coming to stand directly in front of her, his slim frame still opposing as he towered over her. His voice having too quickly returned to that laced with dread tone.

"You are a disappointment. Just like Sherizia," he told her.

Sherizia? His wife.

"She was your wife and the mother of your children. I am your employee," Hailey offered, her body beginning to shake with a mixture of nerves and adrenaline. "I am not like her."

"You were next," Ronnel said through clenched teeth. "You were next for me."

Hailey was shaking her head as he spoke, backing up until her legs hit the bed once more. Jackson had been right all along. Ronnel had been trying to groom her to fill his wife's place. How could she have been so blind?

"I was never here for you," she told him defiantly. "I was here for the job."

His eyes had darkened then, lowering to mere slits across his face as he smirked at her.

"You were here because I allowed it," he told her seconds before he reached out, grabbing her by her throat.

Hailey's hands instantly came up to slap at his. His grip was tight as she felt the pinch of air trying to get to her lungs. His hand clenched tighter around her neck until he'd lifted her off her feet. She still fought, kicking out and slapping at his arms, trying to claw at his face.

"I would have treated you fair. But no, like Sherizia you think you know better. You think you can do better than to be with me. I will show you now," he said in a low, ominous voice. "I will show you!"

Again his tone had shifted from that eerie calm to full blown rage as he yelled into her face, shaking her at the same time. She couldn't breathe. Her eyes were watering as she gasped for air. Still, she tried to fight him, tried to break free of his grasp.

"Let her go," another voice interrupted.

Someone had come into the room but Hailey couldn't see them. Hell, she could barely hear as everything began to shift from clarity to blurriness, sort of like it had in her dream. Only Hailey was positive the white roses weren't going to appear this time.

"She is mine," Ronnel stated through clenched teeth.

He sounded as if the effort to choke her was causing him great emotional strain. Hailey doubted that, but she was feeling dizzy and her attempts to break free had begun to slow. He was killing her. And for what? She hadn't given him any mixed signals. Hell, he hadn't even tried to come on to her in a sexual way. There had been nothing between them that would have given the slightest impression of them being together on another level. She was just his translator, she thought as her eyes rolled back in her head and darkness threatened to overtake her.

"She is the money we need to get out of this mess you put us in," the other guy added.

The words were stilted, yet the voice was familiar, dragging through her mind as Hailey felt her body going limp, her movements ceasing without any direction from her.

There was someone else here, she thought even as her eyes closed, the pain in her neck and the burn in her lungs so strong she could do nothing else but surrender.

In the distance, far across a field of dead grass, on a day as gloomy as the one when her grandparents had come to the school to pick her up and tell her that her parents were dead, Hailey tumbled and fell. She blinked and tried to focus but there was nothing, no one to see. The roses were gone, the feeling of happiness lost. And then there was a sound. It was loud and she wanted to open her eyes to see what it was or who it was making that horrendous noise. She could not.

It was over, she thought, just before hearing another sound—a gunshot.

"It's over," Jackson said the moment he walked into Jerald's office, slamming the door behind him.

Jerald looked up to see his brother striding angrily across the floor, coming to a stop and taking a seat in one of the guest chairs across from his desk.

"Mendoza refuses to meet with us. In much less colorful language than his assistant deemed to use, he's basically telling us and our offer to go to hell," Jackson continued. "I think he has another buyer. One of his friends or someone that will keep him in a leadership role. A quiet one as they're probably planning to wait until the heat from the authorities dies down. But at least he'll still be in charge."

"He'll be in jail," Jerald added. "How's he going to be in charge if he's going to be in jail?"

"You sure about that?" Jackson asked. "I've never known the Feds to take their time arresting someone when they had all their ducks in a row."

"When they're dealing with a global company and people connecting to an international human trafficking ring, I think they like to make sure those ducks are shined up and standing in pristine order before they go kicking in the door," Jerald told him.

He dropped the pen he'd been holding as he was going through the customized terms of employment he was prepared to offer Hailey. She'd been on his mind first thing this morning when he'd awakened. Her and the fact that all his videos had been stolen from his home and there hadn't been any signs of forced entry at all. He'd had a locksmith come over immediately to change all his locks and threatened to personally go down and strangle the president of the security company that had installed the bullshit system which obviously had not worked. The only reason that Mendoza had even been remotely on his radar this morning was, the man Hailey had seen last night. Jerald had been certain he was also Filipino and was probably working on behalf of Mendoza to keep an eye on Hailey. That made him all the more adamant about getting her out of there, today.

Now, it appeared, he would have something else to address with this morning.

"Whatever the case, he's not communicating with us any longer. We've lost the deal." Jackson rubbed a hand over his chin, his brow drawn as he glared at Jerald.

"We've lost deals before," he told him, refusing to show the obvious agitation that his brother was.

"Not like this," was Jackson's quick retort. "Not in this way."

Jerald sat back in his chair then, eyeing his brother suspiciously. "In what way is that?"

"Look," Jackson sighed. "He's a bastard, we both know that. And by tipping the Feds off to all the other dirt we dug up on him, we gave them everything they needed to put the nails in his coffin. We were doing our jobs and our civic duty."

Jerald sighed because he could see where his brother was coming from. This hadn't been an ordinary deal for them. They'd known who and what they were dealing with and they'd made the decision to win both ways with this guy. Only now, it didn't look like that was going to happen.

"Okay, let's just take a moment here to regroup. Let's get the files in here and go through everything once more. I talked to that guy Bonner last night and he's supposed to be here—" Jerald paused, twisting his wrist so he could look down at his watch. It was almost eleven in the morning. "In fact, he'd said first thing in the morning. Guess he's allowing for the time difference. Anyway, we can go through our files, reassess our offer, and we can have Bonner contact D&D's source with the Feds to find out when they're going to arrest Mendoza. Then we can both go see Mendoza and make a last pitch to him. This time we'll talk about his daughters, how he needs to think about securing something for their future."

Jackson nodded. "Yeah, you're right. But I don't know how much of a priority his daughters are to him. Did you notice he didn't even come to the hospital the day of the brick incident?"

Jerald was already picking up his phone to summon Noble into the office, when he looked over at his brother with a nod of his head. "I noticed," he told Jackson. Then to Noble, "Bring me everything we have on Mendoza."

"Wait a minute," Jackson was saying as Jerald hung up the phone. "Did you say Bonner?"

Jerald had already begun stacking the papers he'd been working on, preparing to put them into a folder so he could keep them safe and private while they delved into the business at hand.

"That's what he said his name was. I've been emailing D&D outside of corporation business in an attempt to find out who threw a brick at my back," Jerald admitted.

"But we always deal with Trent Donovan. I've talked to his partner Sam Desdune a couple of times. Sam's sister, Bree, and Trent's cousin, Bailey, also work there. They've done some of the background checking for us."

"I know," Jerald said. "I see the invoices, remember?"

"Right, but I've never dealt with Bonner. He's never done any work for us."

Jerald came to a stop then, a bad feeling landing softly on his shoulders. "So what are you saying? He doesn't work for D&D?"

Jackson shook his head. "No. He's definitely affiliated with them. Well, with Trent, at least. He's a freaking ex-ops Navy SEAL that goes by the name of Devlin "Death" Bonner. I hear he's one bad ass—"

"They're gone!" Noble interrupted as he rushed into the office.

"What's gone?" Jerald asked more than a little agitated by the way his assistant had come into the office without knocking. The last thing he wanted was for Noble to overhear them speaking about Navy SEALS and private investigators. Or the reason why they were talking about such. Noble had been a little more in pocket since the brick incident, questioning Jerald about where he was going and when he would return. The guy had even suggested that maybe Jerald should get a bodyguard. Jerald had ignored that and accepted that his assistant was concerned for his safety. But he didn't like breaches in protocol, not at all.

"All of the files," the guy said.

Today he was wearing an extremely bright pink shirt with a slim turquoise and white striped tie. The vivid ensemble was in stark contrast to the dark black and gray suits Jerald and Jackson were wearing.

"When you were working on them I had them in that bin right beside my desk so that they would be easily accessible. When Jackson returned, DeMarco came down to retrieve them. I just called him and he said that Mandi came to get them the other day saying that you and Jackson requested she bring them to you," Noble told them.

Jackson nodded as he sat up in the chair. "The day we went to the hospital. She came to your house that afternoon and we worked on the files."

"Okay, so call Mandi and tell her to bring the files in here," Jerald told Noble who was already shaking his head.

"She's not here," Noble announced, his lips upturned slightly as if he were thoroughly disgusted. "She called out yesterday and today saying she had a stomach flu or something. I didn't think anything of it because to tell the truth that girl is a pain every second of the eight hours a day she's here." He straightened his glasses after giving Jerald a pointed look. "I can try calling her at home or I can just go over there and pick them up myself."

More protocol breaches, Jerald thought as he massaged his throbbing temples. Files were only to leave the office in the hands of the executives, or by specific direction from an executive. Jerald hadn't told Mandi to bring those files to him and truth be told, with all that had been going on, he'd just assumed that Noble had since his assistant had been like a drill sergeant ordering the intern around since the day she started.

"Yes," Jackson said adamantly. "Go get the damn files."

Noble looked shocked at Jackson's stern voice and deferred to Jerald—which wasn't a good move—for his direction. Even though Jerald was his immediate supervisor and the CFO of the company, Jackson was the CEO, nobody other than their father had more control at Carrington Enterprises.

"Now, Noble," Jerald said as a follow up. "I want those files on my desk within the hour."

Noble nodded and turned immediately to leave.

"Problems with your staff," a deep, husky voice asked a moment after Noble was gone.

Jerald and Jackson hadn't even had a chance to comment on the new developments before a guy that looked like he should be lifting cars or possibly wearing some sort of superhero costume slowly entered the office.

The Carrington brothers both immediately stood, as if their six foot two and six foot three inch heights were any comparison to this guy who was clearly towering over them.

"This is a private office," Jerald had begun saying.

"Devlin Bonner," Jackson interrupted his brother. "It's a pleasure to meet you in person. I'm Jackson Carrington."

The guy had come all the way into the office by that point, stopping just a few feet from where Jackson stood. He wore all black, cargo pants tucked in steel-toed boots and a t-shirt that definitely gave him a body-builder persona. His head was bald, his skin dark and taut over his bulging muscles. The scar on the left side of his face was long and vicious looking and lent credence to the nickname Jackson had mentioned only minutes before—"Death".

Bonner looked down at Jackson's outstretched hand a second before taking it in a stiff shake. Then he looked to Jerald.

"And you're Jerald," Bonner stated. "We spoke last night."

Jerald nodded. "We did. You're late."

"No," Devlin stated. "You are. The Feds arrested Mendoza and his partner an hour ago."

Jackson cursed and Jerald was frowning when his cell phone vibrated on his desk. Snatching it up quickly he answered without checking the caller ID.

"You gotta come quick! There're strange men here and Hailey's hurt or something. She's not waking up. The ambulance is coming but there're so many people and they're all over the place. I don't know what else to do!"

"I'll be right there," Jerald said the moment Malaya had stopped talking. The little girl was hysterical so most of her words had been a jumble of English and Filipino, but Jerald had heard one thing loud and clear. Hailey was hurt.

CHAPTER 10

Both Bonner and Jackson were somewhere behind
Jerald. He'd shouted that something had happened at the
Mendoza house as he'd been on his way out of the office,
not stopping again until he was in the garage and behind
the wheel of his car. He drove through midday traffic not
giving a damn about the possibility of getting pulled over.
Malaya had said the paramedics were there and that Hailey
wouldn't wake up. Nothing else was important to Jerald,
not at this moment.

He made it to the Mendoza estate in twenty minutes.
Unlike the other times he'd had occasion to be here he
turned into the gates that were already open, driving
straight up to the roundabout driveway where police cars,
an ambulance and two black SUVs with federal license tags
were already parked.

Jerald jumped out of his car the second he'd put it in
park, pushing the door closed behind him as he ran to the
front door. Malaya was right there waiting for him.

"She woke up!" the little girl said happily. "She's
upstairs but she woke up!"

Jerald pulled Malaya to him in a tight hug. "Are you
okay?" he asked. "What happened?"

Malaya was shaking her head when she pulled away
from Jerald, a long dark haired ponytail swishing behind
her.

"We were asleep and then there was all this yelling. And then shots and people were everywhere," she told him all in one breath.

Dried tears streaked her face and after she'd pulled her arms from around him, she'd twisted her hands in front of her, nervously. "I'm glad you're safe, Malaya. Now I have to go and see about Hailey."

"She's awake!" Malaya yelled again. "She is!"

He stood then looking towards the stairs. "Is she up there?"

Malaya nodded.

"Where's your sister?"

Malaya shrugged.

Jackson and Bonner had come through the door at that moment and Jerald immediately nudged Malaya over in his direction. "Here keep her with you," he told his brother. "I'm going up to find Hailey."

Jackson looked perplexed but Jerald didn't care, he headed for the stairs, only to hear footsteps behind him. He didn't look back until he'd reached the top of the landing, not bothering to frown as Bonner stepped up behind him.

Jerald had no idea where Hailey was, so he followed the sound of voices down a winding hallway. He didn't see her at first, when he attempted to push his way through the room. The two black suit wearing guys that had been at the door immediately grabbed his arms to stop his progress.

"Get off me!" he yelled at them. "I want to see her!"

"Who the hell are you?" one of the men asked. "This is a crime scene now, sir."

"He's with me," Jerald heard Bonner tell one of the guys.

The guy looked to Bonner who had appeared in the doorway—his bulky frame taking up a good portion of the space to be exact.

"Bonner," the guy said. "What brings your ugly face out of hiding?"

Bonner's reply held no warmth or humor, in comparison to the other guy that had actually seemed happy to see him.

"He's my client," was all Bonner had said before the other guy nodded and released his hold on Jerald's arm.

Giving a look to his partner, the other black suit released Jerald as well. Not really caring at the moment what had just transpired between those three, Jerald turned immediately. He rushed across the room to where paramedics surrounded the bed. When one turned to reach for something in one of their many bags, Jerald slipped into their spot and gasped as he looked down at Hailey.

She looked so frail, her face pale, hair wild around her head. They had an oxygen mask covering her nose and mouth and a woman on the other side had just capped a tube of blood and pulled a rubber wrap from Hailey's arm.

"She's stable," one of the paramedics looked up to tell him.

Jerald didn't bother to acknowledge the words because stable didn't mean a damned thing when he could see the violent purple bruise around her neck. His fists clenched at his sides, teeth gritting.

"We should take you in for observation, Ms. Jefferson."

Hailey was immediately shaking her head. "No," she told them. "Tell them I'm alright, Jerald. That I don't need to go to the hospital."

This was the first time she'd looked over to him so Jerald wasn't sure how she'd known he was there. But when her hazel eyes rested on him and when her words sounded like an immediate plea, there was nothing he could deny her. Not a damned thing.

"If there are signs to look out for, I can do that," he told the paramedics. "And I'll bring her straight to the hospital if anything changes."

"I can't make you go," the paramedic said. "But you may have some dizziness, blurred vision, even trouble swallowing for a day or so." The woman then looked to Jerald and said, "She needs to stay hydrated and to try to get something on her stomach. Other than that plenty of rest should have her feeling better in a few days."

"That bruise is going to hurt like hell in the next couple of days. Cold compresses will help. If you need a prescription for pain you'll need to come back to the ER," the female paramedic that had just taken her blood said.

"I'll be fine," Hailey told them, this time removing the mask from her face. "As soon as I get out of here I'll be just fine."

She began trying to lift up off the bed and the female paramedic touched one of her shoulders.

"Take it easy," she warned her. "You've been through quite an ordeal, Ms. Jefferson. Just lay here for a while."

"No," Hailey said shaking her head. "I can't stay here another minute. I want to leave. Now."

She'd looked up to Jerald and once more he felt the need to do whatever she asked.

"I hear you," he told her, taking her hand in his. "Let's give them a minute to get their stuff together. I'll sit with you and then we'll leave alright?" he asked while easing onto the bed beside her.

Hailey nodded, keeping her fingers twined tightly with his. "I don't want to stay here anymore," she told him. "I'm ready to leave."

Her voice cracked on that last word and Jerald thought his heart would break into pieces right at that moment.

"You don't have to stay, sweetheart. I'll get you out of here. I promise."

It took a few more minutes for the paramedics to gather all their belongings and to go over the warning signs one more time. The agents that had tried to stop him coming in along with Bonner still guarded the door.

"He tried to kill me," Hailey said softly and for the first time Jerald realized how raspy her voice sounded.

"Ms. Jefferson, I am Agent Young from the FBI. I'm sorry we have to meet under these circumstances, but we need a statement from you."

Agent Young was the one that Jerald figured was Bonner's contact with the Bureau. It certainly would explain the look the two of them shared when they'd arrived.

"Not right now," Jerald replied the moment Agent Young stepped towards the bed.

"It's better if they get her side of the story while it's still fresh in her mind," Bonner interjected.

Jerald was really beginning not to like this guy.

"I don't give a damn what you think is better. She's not ready to do this," he said.

"No. I am ready," Hailey replied from beside him. "I want to tell them what happened. I want to get it over with."

Bonner didn't budge but Agent Young nodded to Jerald with a definite smirk. Someone else Jerald didn't care too much for at the moment.

"Start from the beginning, Ms. Jefferson and tell me as much as you can. We'll go as slow as you need. Would you like a glass of water?" Agent Young asked her.

Hailey was about to shake her head, but Jerald chimed in. "Yes. She'd like a glass of water."

The room went silent until Bonner cleared his throat and motioned for the other agent to go and get the water.

"I woke up and he was here," she began. "Right at the foot of the bed."

She continued until Jerald wanted to leap off that bed and find wherever they were keeping Mendoza so he could beat his ass! But Hailey was holding his hand, gripping it tighter when she told of how Mendoza had called her a slut then began choking her.

"Another guy came in and then I heard a gunshot. I was out after that," she said. "I thought I was…dead."

Her last word thrust the room into stunned silence once more and Jerald ignored the fact that they were not alone. He leaned over to kiss Hailey's forehead and used his other hand to rub over her head and down to her shoulders.

"We had to shoot him to get him off you," Young told her gently. "The other guy that came in was Peary Ramirez. He's a recruiter."

The last was directed at Bonner whose facial expression remained grim.

"That means he was here to take her to their network of buyers," Jerald said hating how the words sounded in his voice.

Young nodded tightly.

"Mendoza will get medical care and then he'll be transported to our field office for processing. Ramirez is on his way to the office now," he told them.

"What about his daughters?" Jerald asked thinking of the fear he'd heard in Malaya's voice over the phone and the still haunted look she had when he'd come through the door. "What will happen to them?"

"If they're not U.S. citizens, they'll be sent back to their home country. If they are, then they'll be put in foster care."

The other agent had returned with the water. Jerald handed it to her and Hailey took a tentative sip before saying, "That's horrible for them. This is all so horrible."

"But it's over now, sweetheart," Jerald told her. "We're going to get your things and then we'll leave. I'm going to take you home."

Home.

Jerald had a home and he was certain Hailey did too, in Virginia.

"I'll go to a hotel," she told him.

He didn't argue, not while Bonner and Young were still in the room. He simply nodded and began to help her from the bed. When he pulled back the sheets and realized she was barely dressed he turned to the others with a frown.

"A little privacy, please?" he asked.

Young and the other agent nodded in turn, leaving without another word. Bonner stood staring at him.

"I'll be right outside," he told Jerald.

"I'm afraid of him," Hailey said the moment they were alone.

Jerald had managed a half smile at that. "I'm sure you're not the only one," he told her. "Come on, let's get you dressed so we can find you a hotel."

CHAPTER 11

This was the last place Jerald wanted to be. He'd actually planned to be holding Hailey in his arms at least until noon. Then he'd figured on ordering lunch in and maybe a lazy afternoon watching movies—movies that she liked, not like the ones that had gone missing from his penthouse. But Hailey had other ideas.

"I'm not going to sleep with you tonight, Jerald," she'd said once they'd gotten her settled in the hotel room and had ordered room service for dinner.

They'd just finished the meal and were sitting on the couch in the sitting area of the suite Jerald had booked at the Beverly Wilshire.

"I haven't asked you to," he said feeling a bit offended that she would jump to that conclusion.

While he'd be the first to admit that the start of their relationship had been based on an undeniable lust, Jerald was fully aware that it had quickly turned to something more. Only, he still wasn't ready to put a name on what that something more was.

"I've just been through so much since coming to L.A.," she continued. "I feel like I've been living someone else's life. I've never even thought of going to a sex club before and surely never assumed my first real job in my chosen field of study would lead to someone trying to kill me. It's a bit surreal."

He'd been able to relate to that.

"Sometimes things happen that you could have never imagined," he replied thinking back to his infamous skiing accident. "But the days do get better."

That last sentence came out before he could think to stop it. He hadn't been very optimistic after is accident, a fact that had led to the secluded way he chose to live his life. The life he'd never thought of changing, until Hailey. That's what he'd meant by the days getting better, because he planned for those days to be filled with everything she needed. If he also planned for them to continue their relationship the way it was, well, he didn't need to mention that right now.

She'd leaned forward, resting her elbows on her knees and rubbing her hands down her face.

"I know they will. I just need to take a few seconds to regroup. I'm so worried about my grandmother and now all this is…it's just been a roller coaster ride these last few weeks," she said.

"I've arranged for your medical insurance to go into effect immediately. All you have to do is fill out the forms and I can have my assistant send those over tomorrow," he told her.

"Not just the cancer," she began, staring out towards the window. "Although I guess the other will go away now that Ronnel's in custody."

Jerald frowned at the mention of that man's name. "You guess what will go away?"

"Oh," she said turning to him. "I hadn't told you that someone had broken into my room earlier yesterday and left a message on my phone. It was to my grandmother, apologizing for putting her life in danger. I guess it was Ronnel and I should have told the FBI."

She moved like she was about to stand. Jerald stopped her with a hand to her arm. "It's okay," he told her. "Sit down. I put one of Agent Young's cards on the table over there. He gave Bonner a stack of them before we left the house."

"And this Bonner guy works for you? Is he FBI too?"

"No," Jerald said shaking his head. "That's a long story. But right now I want you to tell me about the threat against your grandmother."

"It was nothing," she told him. "Well, I came to the conclusion that it was nothing because when Ronnel typed the message on my phone, he neglected to send it. I've talked to my grandmother and she's just fine. I guess he figured that would scare me into doing whatever he said. He also took the keys to the SUV which was probably punishment of some sort as well."

Jerald listened to her words but wasn't actually connecting the same dots that she apparently had. Ronnel Mendoza made his threats face-to-face, as noted by the scars on her neck. He wouldn't do something as sneaky as the cell phone incident, it just wasn't his style.

"It's over now," he'd told her, keeping his thoughts to himself.

Bonner had come here because of all the incidents that Jerald had laid out for him. This would be another piece he'd throw at the Navy SEAL to see if he could fit into one big crystal clear picture.

"Yes. It is," Hailey had said to him. "And while I know this is going to sound crazy considering what just happened I think I'd like to be alone tonight."

That had sounded crazy to him because the last thing Jerald wanted to do was leave her alone. On the other hand, he'd never begged a woman before in his life and he wasn't about to start now.

"If you're sure that's what you want," he'd told her after a moment's hesitation.

She'd nodded. "I'm sure. I just need some time with me, to get my thoughts together and figure out what my next step is." She'd held up a hand the second he was about to speak, stopping him cold. "I'm aware of your offer, Jerald and I appreciate it. I just need to take some time to come to my own decisions about all this. So I'll see you tomorrow? Okay?"

No it was not okay, Jerald thought. But wasn't he used to things not being okay in his life?

So he'd agreed and he'd left the hotel room, hating every step he took that led him further from her. What if Mendoza had other men working for him? Others that knew his plans for Hailey? What if he had somehow gotten a message to them to grab her and continue on with the plan? Jerald's mind was whirling with 'what ifs' when Bonner stepped from around a corner in the hotel hallway, startling the crap out of Jerald.

"Do you ever make a sound when you approach? Maybe you should carry some keys in your pocket or something," he said irritably.

Bonner had only frowned back at him as if he had no interest in what Jerald was saying.

"I'll stay here and watch her tonight," the guy announced.

"You'll what? Why? Is there a reason for her to continue to be watched? Did Mendoza escape?" he asked immediately.

"No," Bonner said with a shake of his head. "But there is something that is not right. Something that does not fit."

Exactly what Jerald had been thinking when she told him about the cell phone message.

"I think you may be right," he told Bonner.

The bigger man nodded. "So I'll stay here tonight and then check-in with you in the morning."

"That's a good idea," Jerald said. "What about the morning" How will we keep an eye on her if you're at my office with me?" he asked when he'd been about to walk away.

"Young and Westbrook want to talk to her again about things she may have seen or heard while in Mendoza's house. They'll be here at ten. When they arrive I'll come see you. I'll have them call me when they are about to leave and I'll circle back here to watch her again."

It sounded like a good plan. It also sounded like what Hailey had just said, a roller coaster ride.

Jerald hadn't gotten much sleep last night thinking about Hailey and all that she'd said to him. He'd also been thinking about how he could possibly make this better for her.

In the morning he'd come in to work and sat in his closed office not doing one scrap of Carrington Enterprises work. Instead his mind had been whirling with questions for Bonner as he waited impatiently for the man to arrive. At ten fifteen Bonner called to say that the agents had to switch their meeting to the afternoon. And so it was that at three fifteen Jerald and Bonner were just sitting in his office talking.

"I don't think Mendoza was behind the brick throwing, the cell phone, or stealing those videos from your house," Bonner stated plainly after Jerald had filled him in or what Hailey had told him last night.

Sitting back in his chair Jerald was not surprised by the man's words. After going over everything more than a dozen times last night, Jerald had concluded that he didn't think so either.

"It seems too personal," Jerald said. "Mendoza just met Hailey about six to seven weeks ago. She said he answered an ad she'd put online. He flew her out here for the interview and she'd had a week to go back home, pack and return."

Bonner sat with his legs spread, hands braced on his knees. He wore all black again, this time jeans, another t-shirt and a lightweight jacket that Jerald wondered if he'd only put on to conceal the gun he was almost positive the man was carrying.

"Hailey was a commodity to him. All females are. That's why the authorities are working double-time to find out if his daughters are U.S. citizens or not. They want to get them as far away from Mendoza and his people as possible, before they end up on the market as well," Bonner said.

"So he wouldn't bother to pull up to a salon and toss a brick through a window. Hell, he hadn't even bothered to come down to the scene or to the hospital to check on his daughters," Jerald commented.

"Like I said, commodities. When one is gone they can easily be replaced by another," were Bonner's next words.

Jerald nodded. "He's a filthy bastard and I hope they give him a year in prison for every second of torture women have faced because of him."

"They're certainly going to try," Bonner added. "But that doesn't sew up your problem so neatly. I think what you and Hailey have got is a stalker."

"A stalker?" Jerald said only seconds before his office door swung open.

"Jerald Carrington?" a man wearing a dark and wrinkled suit said as he walked in.

Two uniform LAPD officers came in behind him.

Jerald immediately stood and so did Bonner, his stance that of a man ready for battle.

"Detective O'Hurley," the man in the suit said as he approached, flipping his badge so quickly all Jerald had seen for certain was a flash of silver. "I'm here to ask you about someone that was working for you. Mandi Waters."

"Yes," Jerald said wondering why Noble hadn't called him before letting the officers barge into his office. "She's an intern. Is there a problem."

"How long has she been working for you, sir?" O'Hurley continued in a brisk manner, flipping back his notepad with exaggerated force before he began scribbling.

"Since the beginning of the summer. The end of May I do believe," Jerald answered. "Do you mind telling me what all this is about?"

"It's about a murder," one of the officers that stood near the door like they were blocking an exit spoke up.

"Murder?" Jerald said. "Mandi?"

"Yes and yes," O'Hurley stated coolly. "We've got a witness that clocks her leaving the Elite building yesterday at five. Your name's on the lease to a penthouse there."

The other officer snickered and Bonner gave him a warning look that would have intimidated Superman.

Jerald straightened his tie and kept his eye on the officers while he reached into his top desk drawer slowly. The two officers standing behind the detective reached for their guns. Bonner reached for his.

"Hold on a minute there," O'Hurley said moving his hand slowly beneath his jacket for his gun as well. "Who are you and do you have a permit for that weapon, son?"

"U.S. Navy SEAL and yes, I've got several permits for several guns," he hissed.

"There's no need," Jerald said. "I was just getting a card." He came from around the desk then, offering the card to the detective. "This is my lawyer. Call him with the rest of your questions."

Jerald proceeded to walk across the floor of his office standing for a second to stare at the officers who still acted as if they weren't going to move. After a brief stand-off and another sound from behind Jerald which he figured was Bonner letting them know that he wasn't afraid to use his weapon either, they moved out of his way.

Swinging the door open Jerald stepped out calling to his assistant, "Noble, why didn't—"

He paused because Noble was not there.

"You looking for another one of your employees, Noble King?" O'Hurley asked coming out of the office behind Jerald.

"Yes," Jerald replied.

"We are too. Seems that after Mr. King, while helpful enough to tell us where Mandi was last seen yesterday, neglected to give us a reason as to why his company ID card was found in her hand."

Jerald didn't know what to say. Had Noble killed Mandi? Of course not, Noble wasn't that type of guy. He went to parties on the weekends, came in on Monday mornings telling DeMarco how much fun he'd had and about what "foine" guy he'd managed to bring home with him. He was a playboy, making excellent money, living and loving his single lifestyle. The first thing he was not, was a heterosexual which immediately discounted the possibility that something could have been going on between Noble and Mandi. The second, Jerald thought as he looked over to Noble's desk which was like Jerald's in perfect order, was a murderer. Jerald would stake his life on that, or at least he would have if Bonner had not come barreling out of the office next.

"We've gotta go. Hailey's gone and the agents have no clue where she is," he said causing Jerald's frown to deepen.

This was it.

Adrenaline pumped through my body like a supernatural drug. I couldn't stop it and wasn't certain I wanted to. I mean, I'd always been certain before. From the time I was seven years old I knew—I denied it for a while, but I knew.

I was different.

I played baseball, loved to play baseball actually. And I played with model cars. Well, I helped my dad put them together and I enjoyed looking at the completed project. It brought me closer to him, even though I knew deep down inside that he would never accept me, not the real me.

I was fifteen the first time I kissed a boy. Sixteen, three months and five days when I had sex with one.

What I'm feeling now almost matches what I felt that day. No, it surpasses it.

And it's all thanks to Mandi Waters. That pitiful little tramp. I tried to tell her she was barking up the wrong tree, that there was no way a man like Jerald Carrington would ever be interested in her, but she hadn't listened. In fact, she'd been stupid enough to say the wrong thing to me, the worst thing anyone had said to me in a very long time. So it was her fault. Yes, it definitely was her fault and that little bitch got exactly what she deserved!

"Mr. Carrington was very appreciative yesterday. I think he likes my initiative," Mandi had said after letting me into her apartment.

"Office protocol states that no files should leave the building without the express permission of an executive," I told her as I closed the front door to my apartment behind me, switching the lock into place without her even realizing it.

"No harm, no foul," she said turning around and waving her hand at the dinette table where the files in question were stacked. "I was going to bring them back early this morning but my stomach was acting funny."

She frowned and it wasn't a pretty picture. This chick wore so much make-up I could barely tell who she was without it. She had pimples on both her cheeks, a trio of them that, along with those thick framed glasses she was wearing made her look like a dorky teenager. Her robe had the nerve to be the same fuzzy pink material as her slippers—a cotton candy explosion that was making my stomach act funny.

"Jerald and Jackson were looking for them. Apparently the deal is on the rocks and they wanted to figure out a way they could possibly salvage it. But you messed up that plan," I said.

I'd walked further into the one room apartment, surveying the sparse and tasteless furniture, sniffing the candle-scented air. On second thought, I figured I'd better not sniff too deeply, whatever germs she was carrying were most likely floating around in this room.

"Oh, I didn't know," she said. "Well, here they are. If you just give me fifteen minutes I can get dressed and go into the office with you."

"That won't be necessary," I told her. "You're fired."

She had the audacity to get teary eyed, as if she thought that bullshit was going to work with me. I walked closer to her, clicking my tongue. "There, there, now. Let's not make this anymore uncomfortable than it has to be."

"But I was trying so hard," she said, sniffing back those ridiculous tears. "He was impressed with me, with my work. He told me so when I was at his house."

His house, I thought as I continued to move toward her. I knew that place well. The top penthouse suite in The Elite building on Sunset Boulevard. Jerald owned the entire eighteenth floor. The decorations had been a little bland for my taste, but I could see how Jerald would enjoy the seamless blend of warm colors and sleek furniture designs. The two levels were impeccably neat with a place for everything and everything in its place. Just as I would have it. We were kindred spirits that way, Jerald and I.

We were meant to be together.

It was time this trick got that fact through her head once and for all.

"You should have listened to me," I told her, lifting a hand to touch the disgusting fluffs of her robe.

She licked her lips quickly, took a deep breath and had the bad taste or daft thought—which one I would never be quite certain—to poke her breasts out and tilt her head to the side.

"I don't want to lose this job," she told me. "Isn't there some way we could work this out."

I laughed. I mean, I tossed my head back and laughed harder than I had at the last Kevin Hart stand-up show. Was she serious? Did she really think I would for one minute consider sleeping with her tired looking, skanky ass? Not in a million years or for a million bucks!

The laughter died as quickly as it had come and before I knew it both my hands were on her face, cupping her cheeks tightly.

"I told you he wasn't for you," I said, my teeth clenched because she'd thoroughly pissed me off with this last little stunt. "He's too good for your wanna-be-Julia Roberts ass!"

"He liked me," she said tilting her chin up. "And you know what? I don't give a damn if you don't!"

She pushed me then, taking me by surprise so I stumbled back a few steps.

"Take the stupid files and get the hell out of my house!" she yelled.

"Sore loser," I said with a smile and moved to the table about to reach for the files.

I knocked over a bag instead and all sorts of junk spilled out like scissors, rolls of ribbon, and balloons. What was she about to decorate her house with this stupid stuff? I shook my head and looked back at her just as she said, "No. I'm not the sore loser, Noble. You are."

"What did you just say?" I asked, my entire body going still with her words.

"You've been jealous of me since the day I walked through the door of Carrington Enterprises. At first I wondered why. I did everything to try to get you to change towards me, to see that I was really a good worker. But you stayed on my ass, nitpicking about every little thing from my earrings to my toenail polish, to the way I put stamps on a freakin' envelope!"

My hands fisted at my sides. "You didn't belong there, I said.

She shook her head. "Oh, I belonged there alright and I was the one whose ass Jerald stared at, not yours." She chuckled then. "Yeah, I knew. Christina from the copy center told me when I was bitching about you one day. She said she'd heard you and DeMarco talking about how you wanted to fuck Jerald. How you thought you were going to be the one he finally committed to. Even your best friend thought you were crazy for looking Jerald's way."

"Shut up," I said slowly, my body shaking with rage now.

"He told you that Jerald was definitely not gay but you refused to believe him. And when you found out he was going to that sex club you thought you could get a membership there and end up in his bed. Unfortunately, while The Corporation totally supports the LGBT community, they also respect every member's right to personally select their partners. Jerald never selected you, did he?"

Now she was clicking her tongue. "There, there, Noble, don't cry. You'll find someone like yourself one day. It just won't be Jerald. Even if you fire me," she said with a tilt of her head and a spread of her wide mouth into a smile. "It. Will. Never. Be. Jerald!"

"Shut up!" I screamed and the next thing I knew I was bending down and picking up those scissors.

I charged that silly bitch bringing the scissors down to her chest where it sunk beneath all that pink foolery into her skin. She screamed and I pulled the scissors out of her.

"You bastard!" she said and tried to take a step backwards.

"I said shut up!" I yelled again, driving the scissors deeper into her chest this time.

I did it over and over again, even as her arms flailed and she grabbed at my jacket and my shirt. I kept stabbing her, over and over and over until that silly bitch shut her big, fat mouth!

Then I fell back, my ass hitting the floor, those scissors still in my hands. My bloody hands.

I looked down at my arm, my blue linen blazer from H&M. There was blood on it too. My chest hurt my heart was beating so hard and fast and when I blinked I could swear I saw fireworks. Like there was a celebration going on inside of me, a freedom I'd been waiting to feel.

Well, hallelujah, it was here!

I was here and I knew exactly what I had to do next.

It only took me fifteen minutes to get to my apartment just a block away from Jerald's—the one that took the majority of my paychecks to maintain. But I had to be close to him at all times. I just had to be.

I showered and stuffed my clothes in a black garbage bag. Tomorrow was trash day so it would go out tonight. I was going to miss that jacket even though the suede patches at the elbows were imitation. That was alright, Jerald would buy me nicer clothes, like the ones he wore. No way would he let me continue to shop at bargain stores while he wore tailored suits, Ferragamo ties and Gucci shoes. He would want better for me and I would earn it. I knew all the things to do to keep him happy and satisfied. I just needed the chance to show him.

I deserved the chance to be with him. Especially now.

I left my apartment again intending to head straight back to the office, to tell Jerald and Jackson that I'd knocked on Mandi's door for twenty minutes and received no answer. As I rode down the elevator I thought of exactly what I would say and how I would say it. When I stepped out of my building it was to see a couple arguing.

Him saying something about needing space and her crying, asking how she was supposed to live without him. My heart went out to her and I longed for those scissors once more. I would stab him right in the neck for being a cruel sonofabitch! She'd probably given him everything and that's how he'd shown his appreciation, by walking out of her life. And with that sorry ass line too. My fists clenched as I walked in the opposite direction, willing myself not to turn back.

What if Jerald turned out to be a sonofabitch too? No, he couldn't. He was perfect.

I bet the woman who was now being left by her boyfriend had thought the same thing once upon a time too. She was crying and shaking her head when I chanced a glance back up the street once I'd made it to the corner. I'd parked my car at a meter, away from my building because I didn't want the garage attendant to be able to give the time I'd come back to the building. There was a back entrance that only tenants had a key to and there were no cameras back there, like there were in the front lobby. I knew because there'd been a few nights I'd come back from the club with a hot guy and we'd fucked right there in that little dimly lit hallway. If there were a camera, someone in the hoity-toity building would have snitched by now and I'd have been out on my ass.

At that moment I decided to make a detour and instead walked another two blocks down to a cell phone store where I purchased a burner phone. My mouth spread into a huge grin as I made the first call, whistling while I stood on the sidewalk on hold for the homicide department.

A Detective O'Hurley answered. I told him I was concerned about my co-worker, that she hadn't been seen since she'd left the Elite building yesterday afternoon. He asked if I thought there was foul play and I immediately drew the picture of the intern having an affair with her rich boss. Of course that picture had made my stomach turn and my temples throb, but it had to be done. Just in case Jerald wanted to play games with me after all was said and done.

I was doing this all for him, for us. He'd driven me to it, but on the off chance he was too stupid to understand—like I'd experienced with the other rich guy that I'd given my heart to—then I would be ready for him. My mother always told me to have a plan B.

The next call I made with the phone was to a familiar number and the minute I heard her eager and childish voice answer, I smiled again.

"Hey there, sweetness," I said in my deepest and sexiest voice.

"Oh Noble, I'm so glad you called," she started immediately. "I've been waiting here with the phone in my hand. You said you would pick me up before those FBI men came back. I had to hide in the guest house to avoid them."

"No worries, my love. I'll be there soon," I told her. "Is Hailey there by chance?"

I knew she wasn't but I needed her to be there. I needed her out of the way once and for all.

"No, she's not here. She left with that Carrington guy last night," Rhia told him.

I knew that too.

"Call her and ask her to come over," I instructed the spirited young girl who had given me access to her house and offered me her body, even though the thought of that repulsed me on a couple of levels.

One, she was too damned young. Jail bait, my cousins back in Chicago would have called her. And two, females did nothing for me. Nothing but give me a fucking hard time, instead of a hard-on.

"She won't come back here. I think my father tried to hurt her," Rhia told him. "He was shot you know. Those cops shot him right in Hailey's room."

She whimpered and I rolled my eyes.

"If you call her and tell her you need her I bet she'll come," I continued. "Go ahead, call her Rhia. Call her for me, sweetness. Please."

"But I want you, Noble."

Pity she wasn't the one I needed to want me.

"And I want you too, my sweet," I said tired of spewing niceties at this whining child. "But I'll be just a little longer. So call Hailey and have her come sit with you until I get there."

"You'll come while Hailey is here?" Rhia had asked. "I thought you didn't want to meet her."

"I do now," I told her. "I definitely want to meet her now."

CHAPTER 12

Hailey had taken a cab to the Mendoza estate. She'd never thought she would return here and definitely not so soon but Rhia had sounded desperate. Hailey had thought about them all night, about where they would end up and how they would turn out. This situation was so sad for them. There was no way she would have been able to turn down Rhia's request for her to visit.

Agent Young had called asking if he could come and speak with her again and she'd agreed. They were supposed to come at three. Rhia had called her at one. Hailey figured she had time to run out, see Rhia and then get back to the hotel to meet the agents.

But when she walked into the guest house where Rhia had asked her come, she knew instantly that she wasn't going to make that meeting.

Rhia and Malaya were both sitting on the couch, their hands tied behind their backs, ankles also tied together, duct tape over their mouths. Hailey didn't move, not sure if she should go to them—because what if someone were waiting behind the door and grabbed her as she completely entered the house? She thought about backing away and running, but where would she go? The cab was already gone and she didn't have another vehicle. She was stuck.

No, she thought the moment she heard the click of a gun as the nozzle pressed against her temple, she was screwed.

"There's a GPS chip in her phone," Jerald said to Bonner who had insisted on driving when they left his office building.

"I know," Bonner replied. "I already sent it back to the office. Bailey's tracing it now. She's going to text me as soon as—" he trailed off reaching into his pocket for his phone.

"Why would she go back to the Mendoza house?" he asked.

"What the hell?" Jerald said. "I'm calling Young right now. They need to verify that Mendoza's still chained to that bed at the hospital and that he hasn't had a chance to contact anyone."

Jerald dialed the number but didn't get an answer. He cursed, pressing the OFF button on his phone he feared he'd probably broken it.

"Why would she go back there?" Jerald repeated Bonner's question. Then, as he thought about it more, he said, "The girls."

Bonner frowned, which wasn't a far jump from his normal facial expression. "What girls?"

"Mendoza's girls. She would have wanted to check on them, to make sure they were okay. They've bonded in the time that she's worked there and she's worried about their future," Jerald told him. He knew that what he was saying was correct, but he still wasn't certain that was the crux of this situation. A deep sense of dread slithering down his spine told him it was more.

"We'll be there in five minutes," Bonner said. "Text our location to Young just in case."

"Just in case, what?" Jerald asked not liking the sound of Bonner's statement.

"Just in case it is Mendoza's doing and just in case we need back-up," he said turning sharply onto the winding road that led up the hill to Mendoza's place.

"I didn't think you needed back-up since you came all the way out here by yourself. Where's Donovan anyway?" Jerald asked as he texted.

"He's dealing with some family stuff and no, I usually don't need back-up when I'm the only one going into a mission. But it's a smart move and I'm no fool. Besides, there are civilians involved that I've got to protect."

Made sense Jerald thought. In the wake of all that was going on it was nice to have one thing make sense.

The first thing Jerald noticed when they pulled up to the house was the SUV that Hailey normally drove was pulled up onto the grass, right beside another house on the property. She'd told him last night when they talked about someone being in her room and leaving a message on her phone, that her keys to the truck were gone. She thought Mendoza had taken them, but Jerald wasn't so certain. The man certainly would not have pulled the truck up onto his lawn just to park it.

"What is it?" Bonner asked him once they'd gotten out and he noticed Jerald staring in that direction.

"I don't..." he'd just begun to say when they both heard the ear piercing scream.

Breaking out into a run, Jerald took the lead because he'd been standing closest to the open area while Bonner had been standing in between the vehicles. He came to an immediate stop, almost toppling over when he saw Noble walking out the front door carrying Hailey in his arms.

"What the hell are you doing here?" he asked, the dread that had been trickling down his spine making every muscle in his body go stiff.

Noble looked up to him then, the glasses he normally wore gone, his eyes wide and excitable.

"She's nothing but trouble," Noble told him with an eerie grin. "I knew it the moment I saw her on that video from the island trip. I could tell by the way you looked at her."

"What...how did you know about that?" Jerald asked feeling the second Bonner came up behind him.

"Oh, I know everything you do, Jerald. That's what a good assistant does." He dropped Hailey to the ground then and she moaned.

Her hands and ankles were tied and there was tape sloppily slapped over her mouth.

"I know about your membership at The Corporation too," Noble continued pulling the gun from the front ban of his pants, switching off the safety and aiming it down at Hailey's head.

"At first I was like, 'What the hell? Why does he need to go to that club when I'm right here?'" Noble spoke not even bothering to look down at Hailey but keeping his gaze set on Jerald.

"I joined the club. It took all of my savings and I had to borrow a little but I was able to get a yearly membership. I put my name on the list and described you to a tee in the hopes that you would show up on my profile as a suggested connection. But you never did." Noble shook his head as he smiled.

Jerald knew that smile. Or at least he thought he had. He thought he'd known this guy. But now as he stared at him, at the same six foot tall man with curly hair that he'd watched come and go in his office for the last three years, Jerald saw someone different.

He threw back his head and laughed, sobering only when Bonner stepped a couple feet away from Jerald.

"Keep it still, SEAL," Noble told him, leaning in a little so that he could point the gun closer to Hailey.

She wasn't crying, Jerald noticed. Not one tear had been shed along the smooth skin of her face, but her eyes showed her fear and that pissed Jerald off even more.

"You stalked me?" Jerald asked. "You're the one that broke into my house and stole those videos and you threw that brick at me. Why Noble? Why are you doing all this? What do you hope to accomplish?"

"Accomplish?" Noble asked, his gaze returning to Jerald. "Will you give that work shit a rest for a minute, babe. It's not about accomplishing anything. It's about claiming you. About finally having you the way I've wanted you for so long."

"And what way is that?" Jerald asked incredulously.

"Oooh, I see," Noble said drawing out the 'o' sound and shaking his head. "You want to act like you're in denial. Okay, well I knew that might happen. But that's because she's a distraction. Once I get rid of her…"

Jerald interrupted him. "You threatened her grandmother didn't you? Or you tried. You wanted to scare her so she would leave L.A. You were trying to take her away from me," Jerald said realization hitting him like a heated ball in the pit of his stomach.

It had been Noble all along.

"She's a stupid, young, bitch! She has no idea what she needs to get on with her life, let alone what you need in yours. So yes! I've been trying to make you both see how wrong you are for each other. Now, I've just got to put a stop to this. I'm sick of waiting."

Noble was sick of waiting…for him. Jerald tried like hell to wrap his mind around this entire situation. Noble had wanted to be with him, romantically? In all these years when Jerald was avoiding a committed relationship with any woman, he'd never in his wildest dreams considered a *man* might be interested in him.

"You're a fucking lunatic!" Jerald shouted finally.

Noble smiled. "I'm the lunatic with a gun."

Jerald didn't think. He didn't consider, he didn't pause. He just ran, a guttural yell tearing from his lungs and echoing in the air as he slammed into Noble at the waist. The force of the hit knocked the air out of Noble as he fell to the ground with a grunt, the gun he was holding flipping out of his hand.

Rearing back Jerald punched Noble in the face. When the bastard only laughed, he punched him again and again.

Harder and harder until his knuckles stung and his breaths came in heavy pants.

In his mind all he could see was Hailey with blood on her forehead the day that brick was thrown, Hailey lying on the bed with an oxygen mask on her face, Hailey lying on that ground bound and gagged. His mind screamed as rage tore through his body and his fists moved faster. Noble's laughing had stopped. He'd never bothered to swing back or try to protect himself in any way, but Jerald didn't give a damn he simply kept hitting him, the way he'd also wanted to hit Mendoza and anybody else that dared to hurt Hailey.

On the next swing his arms were pulled back until he howled, his body being dragged back across the ground.

"What the hell are you doing?" Jerald yelled.

"I'm stopping you from being arrested for murder," Bonner stated calmly. The big guy glanced over at Noble who lay bleeding on the ground, still breathing, but barely.

"While there's no doubt the bastard deserves a good ass kicking, you shouldn't be jailed because of his stupidity. Now go tend to your woman. She looks like she needs you right now."

Bonner had turned away then, as if Jerald and Hailey weren't even there. After dragging Noble over to the SUV he opened a door and yanked Noble's arm to cuff it to the steering wheel. Jerald watched him march into the house at that point. Sirens sounded in the distance as Jerald came to a stand and ran over to where Hailey was lying on the ground. He fell to his knees in front of her, taking the tape from her mouth gently.

"Oh my god! How did you know I was here? How did you know to come and get me?" she asked, throwing her arms around his neck the moment he'd untied the rope at her hands.

Jerald hugged her to him, holding her tight, his eyes closed as he rocked her.

"I told you I wanted to help you," he said. "I've always wanted to be there for you, Hailey. Always."

"Oh Jerald," she sighed in his arms. "I'm so glad you came. So glad you're here with me."

"I won't leave you again," he whispered into her hair. "I promise."

"Is it over now?" Hailey asked when they were back in her hotel room.

She sat on the bed, falling back so that she could stare up at the ceiling.

"Noble's in jail for kidnapping you and the Mendoza girls and for killing Mandi. The detective that came to see me earlier today, searched his apartment while Noble was at the Mendoza place losing the last of his mind with us. They found the murder weapon and his bloody clothes," Jerald said.

He sat on the bed too, leaning over to rest his elbows on his knees.

"Wow, I can't believe all of this has happened. It's like a Jennifer Lopez movie," she said trying to keep it light, trying desperately not to think that just a day ago she'd been choked until she was unconscious and today she'd been tied up and held at gunpoint.

"I'm sorry," she heard Jerald say quietly.

"You're sorry? What are you sorry for?"

He sat up then, rubbing his hands down his face. "Noble was on my watch. He was my employee and I had no clue that he was infatuated with me."

"I'd say it was more like he was obsessed with you," Hailey added. "Before you showed up he told me all the things he knew about you that I didn't. All the reasons he was better for you than I was."

"I had no idea he was watching me like that. None at all."

"You had no idea he was watching you but you had no problem taping the women you slept with so that you could watch them," she said without a second thought.

He turned immediately at her words, staring down at her. Hailey had considered being outraged by the fact that there were videos of her having sex. Noble had told her about them before Jerald arrived. Jerald had never mentioned them to her and that pissed her off. Only, after everything had happened, she just couldn't bring herself to be angry about it now. She was simply grateful to be alive.

"I never meant for anyone to see those. There was only one copy and I never would have done anything with them besides keep them for my own personal use," he told her.

"And what's that, Jerald? Why do you need to sleep with women who don't give a damn about you and then tape them and watch the interlude over and over again? What could you possibly gain from such a sordid and lonely hobby as that?"

She'd turned her head so she could see him, as she waited for his reply. Jerald Carrington had it all—he was gorgeous, rich, successful, and popular. He could have any and everything in this world that he wanted and yet each time she looked into his eyes she could feel her heart breaking for him, for the sadness she always saw there.

"It's just what I do," he said turning away from her.

Hailey sat up. She moved to sit beside him, touching a finger to his chin and turning his face to her. "I would like a real answer, Jerald. After all that we've been through together, you owe me that little bit of honesty."

He looked at her for what seemed like endless moments and Hailey actually feared that he wouldn't respond, that he would continue to hold himself away from her. It was a thought she'd had often, one she knew she could never live with.

"When I was nineteen I was in a skiing accident," he said slowly. "There was a spinal injury that left me temporarily paralyzed." He took a deep breath and let it out slowly. "It also left me temporarily impotent."

Hailey's hand dropped from his face.

Jerald nodded as if he'd known saying that would cause some type of reaction from her.

"For almost a year I laid in a bed wondering not just if I'd walk normal again, but if I'd ever get an erection. If I would be able to be with a female again, to please her and myself. It was torture," he said solemnly.

"But it did get better and I moved on. Only that fear never subsided. There was always the 'what if'. 'What if I was with a woman and I couldn't get it up?' 'What if I did get it up and then it just stopped?'"

"Oh Jerald," she finally sighed. "I'm so sorry."

He shook his head immediately. "Don't feel sorry for me. Pity is not what I need. I never needed that."

She touched his knee then, feeling as if she had to reach out to him in some way.

"A couple times a year I would hire professional escorts. We would spend a few nights here and there together and that would be it. When I found out about the club I figured this was a more convenient way to fulfil my needs. I joined and I hired the women of my choice. I slept with them and I taped them. At first it was a way of reminding myself that I'd healed. With each woman that I pleased I considered myself whole. But it was all a lie. I knew that when I left Turks and Caicos. None of those interludes compared to when I was with you."

Hailey hadn't cried when Mendoza had choked her and she hadn't cried when Noble had pointed a gun at her, but now, right at this moment she could feel tears welling in her eyes.

"Nothing that I'd ever experienced could compare to when I was with you either," she confided in him. "It was as if you were my first and there's a part of me that knows there'll never be anyone like you in my life again."

Jerald looked to her as if he hadn't believed her words, but he wanted to.

"I'm flawed," he told her. "I've always known that and I've always been able to accept that. But with you, for you, Hailey, I want to be more, to be better."

She smiled, bringing her hands up to cup his face. "We're better together, Jerald. I think that's why we were so connected to each other. Even when I tried to walk away I always ended up in your arms again. Like fate," she told him.

Like he was the one for her and had been all along, just as she'd told Pops in her dream.

"I want you Jerald Carrington, flaws and all. I want you. Over and over again."

Acting on instinct alone Hailey leaned in to kiss him, whispering how much she wanted him between stroking her tongue over his lips and slanting her mouth over his so she could take the kiss deeper. It was the first time she'd kissed him, the first time she'd been the one to initiate sex between them, the first time she admitted to herself that she'd fallen in love with this man.

"Oh Hailey, you have no idea how good it feels to hear you say that," he replied, turning and pulling her onto his lap, his hands immediately going to the tie-up in the front of her shirt.

She pulled back and let him lift the shirt over her head. "I've never felt like this before," she told him. "Never needed to be touched and taken by someone as desperately as when I'm with you."

Jerald tossed the shirt to the floor and yanked at her bra until her breasts were free. He leaned in instantly, licking along each mound. "Whenever I close my eyes I can feel how soft your breasts are against my face, how sweet the skin is right here," he said licking along the inside of her right breast. "And here," he whispered as his tongue slid along the inside of her left one.

Hailey held his head right there, loving how his mouth felt on her breasts. She lifted one when he'd taken the nipple into his mouth, holding it up to him as if she were feeding him, loving the deep, almost painful sting, of his suckling.

"Yes!" she screamed arching in his arms.

She needed him right now!

Her fingers were quick working over the buttons of his dress shirt. He'd lost the tie as they'd sat in the police station waiting to give their statements. She pushed the shirt off his shoulders and down his arms, then instantly began pulling the undershirt he wore from his pants.

"Stop!" Jerald said adamantly, grabbing her wrists.

The intensity of the word compounded by how tightly he was holding her had worried Hailey and her eyes immediately opened so she could look at him.

"What is it?" she asked.

"Leave it on," he told her, then proceeding to unbutton her pants.

Hailey thought back to each time they'd made love and remembered that Jerald had never been totally naked.

"I want it off," she said grabbing his wrists so that he could not continue to remove her pants.

"It's not a big deal, Hailey," he told her, staring for a few seconds as if his look alone would change her mind.

Hailey scooted off his lap. She toed off her shoes and pushed her pants and panties down and off her legs. Standing before him she was totally naked and horny as hell. But she wasn't playing with Jerald Carrington, not anymore. They'd come too far and gone through too much for him to not give her one hundred percent.

"I want you naked, just as I am," she told him.

"Hailey," he said in a low voice.

"No negotiation. Naked."

His dick was so hard, she could see it tenting his pants and her mouth watered. She couldn't wait to get her hands on him. She loved to feel him in her hands and inside her pussy. But no, she would not give in this time.

"Naked or go," she told him folding her arms over her chest.

"I thought you wanted me," he said coming to a stand.

Hailey had no idea when this woman had arrived to take over her mind and her body but she was here and there was no holding her back. She lifted a leg to rest her foot on the bed, then she pressed two fingers between her legs, circling them over her clit then back to sink into her dripping pussy. She pumped herself quickly until the sound of her arousal echoed throughout the room.

"I do," she whispered. "Can't you hear it?"

A muscle in his jaw twitched.

"All you have to do is get naked and you can have it, baby. You can have it all," she told him.

Jerald lowered his head. "Hailey, you don't understand."

"Make me understand," she said pulling her hands free and touching those two fingers to his lips.

He licked her fingers, lapping at them as if he were dying of thirst. Then he ripped his shirt off, like literally pulled it until it stretched and tore from his body. He grabbed her then, turning her and pushing her onto the bed, lifting her legs up until her ankles rested on his shoulders.

He had his pants unbuckled and down at his ankles in seconds, his thick cock spearing into her before she could murmur his name. Hailey gasped and moaned, she loved how he completely filled her, his thickness stretching her wide and pressing deep inside of her.

"Jerald!" she screamed his name when he pulled out and thrust back in. "Yes!"

He pounded into her mercilessly, until her breasts bounced and slapped against her torso, her head thrashing on the bed. He kept her legs up high, holding her at the hips and making sure she received every long and delicious inch of him.

"Is that what you wanted?" he asked her. "You wanted me to have this pussy didn't you?"

"Yes! Yes, baby!" she cried.

"But you tried to take it from me. You tried to tease me with it."

"Oh no! It's yours Jerald. It's all yours!"

"Yeah!" he groaned, pumping her from a side angle, then jamming into her straight back and forth until her legs trembled, her fingers pulling the sheets from the bed.

"Jerald!"

"Hailey!"

They both screamed as their release took hold, wrapping around them and holding their bodies tight during what felt like a torrential storm ripping through her body.

After a few seconds he leaned forward, letting her legs down gently, before laying on top of her. The second he did Hailey wrapped her arms around him, flattening her hands over his strong back and squeezing him tight. "I…" she began to say but paused.

She moved quickly, pushing him to the side so that she could rise up on her knees. She pressed against his shoulders until he lay on his stomach with no resistance from him. That's when she saw it, the scar stretching up and down his back. With shaking fingers Hailey touched him there, felt the bubbled skin beneath her fingers and ached for him all over again.

"You didn't want me to see your scar," she said softly.

"I said it's not a big deal."

"It is," she told him before leaning in to touch her lips lightly to the top of the scar. "It's a big deal because it's a part of you." She dropped tiny kisses down the length of his spine. "It's a part of you that I've fallen in love with."

Jerald moved then, turning over onto his back and pulling her so that she straddled him. He was hard again and thrust deep into her, holding her hips tightly. Hailey fell forward onto his chest, rotating her hips and riding him until another blissful release.

That's how their night proceeded. Sex, shower, a pizza Jerald ordered somewhere around midnight, more sex and finally dropping off into the deepest, most pleasurable sleep she'd ever had.

In the morning Jerald was gone.

She found a note on the bathroom mirror with instructions for her to come to Carrington Enterprises and meet with someone in Human Resources to find out where she would be working. He also gave her the number to the persons that dealt with the medical insurance and the tuition reimbursement office.

He hadn't even signed the note which was even more telling to Hailey.

She showered and dressed and refused to shed one tear. She'd told him she was in love with him. They'd made love all night, or at least she'd thought it had been making love. But in the light of day she had to face the fact that nothing had changed. Jerald was still the CFO of a nationally successful company, and as such he was pulling all sorts of strings to help her. Hailey should be grateful, she knew. But none of this was what she wanted from him. He could keep his job and his insurance and tuition reimbursement because in the end all she'd wanted was him.

It was clear that he did not want the same thing.

So Hailey knew what she needed to do. She packed her bags and she left the Beverly Wilshire heading straight to the airport and back home where she knew exactly who she was and what she wanted out of life. That was where she did whatever she needed to do to help herself and the thought of being at another rich man's beck and call for the sake of financial security, was a distant memory.

By noon that day she was saying goodbye to L.A. and to Jerald Carrington, forever.

CHAPTER 13

Four Weeks Later

Jerald walked into the Celia's an American and Mexican themed restaurant.

He felt a little out of place and definitely over dressed in his three piece suit and Prada tie-ups that produced a clunking sound as he walked across the wood planked floor to the booth where the hostess had seated him. This had been a long time coming, he thought as he sat not looking at the menu that had been placed in front of him. Four weeks to be exact.

A month ago he'd gone to the Beverly Wilshire straight from work after having learned that Hailey had not come into the office as he'd told her to. The Mendoza deal had been lost but Jackson had moved on to their next acquisition so he'd been in meetings all day. He'd thought of her just as he had every day since meeting her, but he hadn't been able to call her. Imagine his surprise when he arrived at the hotel to find out that she'd checked out. He'd immediately called her, only to receive her voice mail.

That had been the case for the next two days also, until the third day when he called and learned that the number had been disconnected.

She'd left him.

No woman had ever left Jerald before.

"It's time to change your way of thinking, Jerald," his mother had said at the end of week two when he'd been at his parents' house for brunch.

"What?" He hadn't been listening to her or any of the chatter going on at the table.

The only reason he'd gone to the brunch at all was because he'd missed the one last week, not wanting to do anything but go to work and back home. He couldn't even watch the one video he had left of her.

Lydia reached in front of her son. She moved his glass from the right side of his plate to the left. Then she used a fork to take all of the red grapes out of her bowl of fruit salad and placed them in Jerald's bowl.

"What are you doing?" he asked, immediately pushing the bowl from in front of him.

Lydia pushed it back.

"It's time for a change. Move your glass to the other side, eat the grapes that you think look like little eyes. Take a chance, Jerald. That's what you do when you've found the one for you," she told him.

He hadn't wanted to hear her words then and she'd had plenty to say for the next half hour. Celise and Tara had even chimed in with their thoughts on the Hailey situation, all of them coming to the conclusion that he should definitely go after her. That decision—although he had eventually realized it was the right one—had taken days and days to come.

Until the morning he woke up and opened the top drawer of his dresser. He kept all of his underwear there, neatly folded, boxers on one side and undershirts on the other. In between them was a coral colored bikini top.

It was the one Hailey had worn in Turks and Caicos.

She'd left it in the room that night and he'd kept it. He'd folded it and put it at the bottom of his drawer. This morning it was right on top, bright and cheery as the sunny day. And Jerald knew. It was fate, just like she'd said the last night they were together.

He loved that color on her and almost smiled as he looked up from the booth where he was sitting at the restaurant to see her wearing a shirt that very same color, jeans and a black apron around her waist.

She was looking down at the pad in her hand as she approached his table. When she stopped and looked up she had a smile on her face as she said, "Good Evening welcome to…" her words trailed off the moment she saw him.

"Hello, Hailey," he said.

"What are you doing in Virginia?" was her next question.

"I came to see you," he replied.

"Why?"

"Because I missed you."

She shook her head as if dismissing his words. "Would you like to place an order?"

"Yes," he said. "I want you."

She frowned at him. "I'm not on the menu."

"No," Jerald continued. "But you've been on my mind more than any other person, business deal or thought I've ever had."

"You should probably get a new hobby," she snapped. "Change things around and maybe let someone tape you having sex."

Jerald completely understood her hostility. In fact, he'd expected it. Her grandmother had told him she'd been in a surly mood since she'd returned. Jerald liked Katherine Jefferson. He'd gone to her house looking for Hailey first and she was the one that told him her granddaughter was working here. After she'd scolded him for breaking Hailey's heart. She was a vital and exuberant woman, a contrast to the sickly elderly person he'd expected when Hailey had told him about her. And she reminded him a lot of his mother, which is why he'd promised her that he would correct his mistakes and he would make Hailey happy. Finally.

"Can you have a seat so we can talk?" he asked motioning towards the bench across from him.

"I'm working, Jerald. You can't just come in here and start making demands on my time. I need this job," she told him vehemently.

"And I need you," he continued.

Hailey shook her head. "It's not that simple, Jerald."

"It is."

"You don't just get what you want because of who you are and how much money you have. I'm not for sale and I won't be at your beck and call just because you offered me a job and tuition reimbursement."

She was trying to keep her voice down and trying to tell him to get lost. Jerald wasn't going to pay attention to either.

He stood from the bench, taking the pad from her hand and dropping it onto the table. He kept that hand in his even though she'd tried to pull away from him and then he'd gone down on one knee. There was dirt on this floor, Jerald knew that but he didn't care. People had turned around and were now staring at them and he didn't care.

"I offered you a job, health insurance and college tuition," he began speaking as he looked up at her. "And I expected you to accept it all because it was what you said you needed. I wanted to give you everything you needed because I thought that would make you stay with me. I was wrong."

"Jerald," she hissed and pulled on her hand again.

He kept his grip on her and continued, "I told you that what Mendoza had offered you wasn't enough. It has taken me four miserable weeks to realize that my offer to you wasn't enough either. I thought I had my life all figured out and I was going according to that plan. I didn't need or want anything else until you came along. And then Hailey, I don't know when it happened or how it happened, all I know is that the minute I had to sit and consider that I might never have you in my life again, I realized that life wasn't worth a damn."

She was shaking her head, tears welling in her eyes. She'd stopped trying to pull away from him and that had given Jerald hope.

"You asked me what I'm doing in Virginia and I'm here to tell you anything," he said with a shake of his head and his heart in his throat. "I'll give you anything, Hailey. Anything and everything that you need if I can just have you in my life. And before you respond, let me..." he fumbled a bit as he reached into his suit pocket to pull out the black box he'd put there. He didn't want to let her other hand go so he used his mouth to help him open the box so that he could turn it around and present the 15-carat oval shaped diamond ring to her.

"I'm making you a better offer," he continued. "This time I'm offering you my heart. Forever. Please say yes. Please."

She'd lifted a hand to her lips as around them the other customers of the restaurant stared in awe, a couple of them beginning to chant softly, "Please say yes."

Shaking her head as the first tears fell she actually chuckled. "You're going to throw away those pants when you get home aren't you?"

Jerald looked down at the dusty wood floor, then back up at her. "No. If you say yes you'll marry me, I'm going to keep this entire outfit. I'm sure the girls will get a kick out of knowing that it's what I wore when I proposed to you."

"The girls?" she asked.

"I've petitioned for guardianship of Rhia and Malaya. We found out they were actually born here and U.S. citizens. I didn't want them to grow up in foster care."

"But you don't have children. You live a solitary life," she said.

It was his turn to shake his head. "I want to live a life with you. A new and changed life that includes the girls and a new house and room for your grandmother. She wants a hot tub too, she told me before I left her house today." Katherine had told him the hot tub was something she and her husband had wanted all their lives. Since the results of her biopsy had come back and she definitely had mesothelioma, having that hot tub would be a blessing before she departed this life.

Hailey smiled at the mention of her grandmother.

"How long are you going to let me stay on this floor groveling, Hailey? I love you more than life itself but I don't know how long I'm going to be able to ignore the dirt and germs down here."

"But you look so sweet down there," she said with a tilt of her head. "I know, I'll come down there with you."

She was bending to her knees before Jerald could stop her. "Put it on me so I can see if it fits," she said when they were both kneeling.

Jerald smiled then, removing the ring and slipping it onto her finger. Applause sounded and Jerald immediately went in for a kiss.

"I hope you don't regret this," she said, when she'd pulled back from the kiss, resting her forehead against his.

"There are no regrets, Hailey, not as long as I have you."

OTHER BOOKS BY A.C. ARTHUR
WWW.ACARTHUR.NET

Erotic Romance

The Carrington Chronicles
Wanting You (Parts One & Two)
Needing You
Having You

Mystery

The Rumors Series
Rumors
Revealed – *Coming Soon*

Sexy Paranormal

The Shadow Shifters
Temptation Rising
Shifter's Claim
Seduction's Shift
Hunger's Mate
Passion's Prey
Primal Heat

Wolf Mates
2-in-1 Book Title: Claimed By The Mate, Vol. I
(September 15, 2015) The Alpha's Woman, by A.C. Arthur

Made in the USA
Monee, IL
03 September 2024